Trinity

Steven Zizza

DEDICATION

For my Trinity – Melissa, Olivia, and Tres

ACKNOWLEDGMENTS

Special thanks to my editor and mentor, Ann Marie Monzione and illustrator, Lisa McSweeney for helping me realize my goal

CHAPTER 1

Who am I? Call me Zero. Short and to the point, I am no one, an orphaned soul abandoned and forgotten by the inhabitants of a cruel world. My current circumstances have amplified a devastating sense of isolation that extends beyond the metaphysical and into the physical.

Darkness surrounds me. I'm lost, but does anyone know? Is anyone looking for me? I've awakened in a cold and dark place, not understanding how I got here, wherever here is. I try to cry for help, but it's a futile effort. Unable to move my lips and paralyzed by fear, my attempted screams reverberate within me and create a hellish torment that cuts deeply into my body and soul. I beg for someone to find me in the cold and dark world that I now inhabit. I try to scream but no sound can be heard. Hello, hello, is anyone there? I'm here! I'm here! Mother of Heaven, please help me! My torture is endless.

Having been emotionally and spiritually lost all of my life, recent events have brought my existence to its lowest depth. Does anyone care? Of course not, why would they. Damn all of you! What have you done to me? My heart is empty, and I can only refill its void with fury, anguish and futility, my best friends. Encased in a cocoon of immobility, my pain yields conflicting emotions of misery and rage, a bitter recipe for the soul.

Wait…what is that sound? Is that water? Yes, it has to be. It can't be anything else.

From an immeasurable distance, another sound, a haunting voice is calling to me. "Hello, my friend. It seems you have gotten yourself into some bit of trouble. We're so glad to finally meet you." Unintelligible murmurings echo around me.

Panic and confusion consume me now. Emotionally supercharged, I struggle to understand what's being said. I try to wave my arms, thinking that would aid in my rescue, but these efforts are also futile. My body has become lifeless, a seemingly powerless and empty cadaver. Who is calling me? Why can't I see anything or anyone? Is there more than one person out there?

Unable to speak, I struggle to respond. Cries for help continue to reverberate within me. "What do you mean 'we're so glad to finally meet' me?" The garbled murmurs moderate to an almost melodious and seductive tone. Suffocating and drowning in a sea of indifference, the abyss is beckoning me, but why? What does it want? The specter of death invades my thoughts, and an ungodly panic almost asphyxiates me. Was death looking to ferry me across the River Styx? Could this specter hear my thoughts?

Slowly, I regain my faculties to continue my appeal for liberation from this hellish prison. "Hello, are you still there? Can you see me? For some reason, I can't move." Then, like a flash of lightning, painful images come rushing back to me. I remember what happened. There was a fishing trip on a clear and sunny day, sounds of evil laughter and an act of ultimate betrayal committed on me. Those bastards killed me, or I think they did. In an instant, my body and soul are jolted by a physical and ethereal disturbance. My heart races. My eyes are wide open but can't see anything. I scream silently in agony, but no one can hear my cries or see me, which doesn't come as a surprise. No one has ever heard or seen me.

Suddenly, the spectral voice calls out to me again, "Stay calm, Buddy Boy. Stay calm."

I couldn't understand how this phantom of the abyss could hear my thoughts or see me. I began to question my understanding of this situation and place. Perhaps, this is some sort of a virtual reality simulation, or I'm lying comatose in a hospital bed dreaming all of this.

The voice offered no lifeline before dissipating into the distant ether. "Stay calm, Buddy Boy. I see you perfectly. Everything's going to be alright. You're not ready. Trust me. You're not ready."

"Not ready…what do you mean? Why won't you get me out of here?" Adding to this emotional rollercoaster, there was no response to my plea, and a momentary relief at being saved ended abruptly. While my suffering was unrelenting, an odd realization came to me. My tortured soul felt a profound intimacy with the cold and darkness surrounding me. These intimate companions swaddled my body like a new-born baby.

My mind wanders from my present situation to reflecting on old experiences and my pitiful existence. How do you cope knowing your value is nothing to humanity? I am Zero, the absence of value, positive or negative, future, past or present.

I was a stranger to the joys of paradise, limping though life, lost in a sea of alienation and heartaches. Life's beauty was always beyond my reach and potential. A zombie in search of a meal, I staggered through my daily routines seeking sustenance. My pace was slower than those slow-motion replays where the players appeared frozen in time. Life evolved in front of my eyes as the world raced by me. I failed both spiritually and physically through life's daily struggles, understanding that I wasn't worth any love, compassion, or attention. Even when love was given, I knew it wasn't deserved. Why would it be? I am Zero, the ultimate indifference, the void.

Many times, I tried to step beyond my place in life, the spot designated for me by the universe...no one saw me....no one accepted me, an unwelcome member of society, a space filler.

Life had always seemed beautiful to me, even though many people looked like extras from one of the many zombie movies that had become so popular in recent years. Was this an accurate reflection of happiness? I didn't know. I just kept watching, my own personal social experiment.

I was content in the knowledge that I didn't have an impact on the lives of others; or so I thought. I heard their laughter. I saw happiness, a foreign place to find a kernel of joy for sustenance. Sometimes, I heard their pain and wished it were otherwise as no one deserved the anguish I bore each day. I found it suffocating. Could I have helped anyone, perhaps applying an emotional salve to alleviate the stinging of an open wound? Would it have really made a difference?

Then again, impacting the lives of others didn't matter. Didn't I already tell you I am nothing. A Zero trying to participate in daily life is a momentary and unwelcome distraction, a blip in the virtual reality that guides the world with an invisible hand. Zero, by its nature, is unseen, invisible. Any attempt to move past Zero was doomed for failure. I was clumsy. I knew my place. I knew my ugliness. I didn't need a reminder. The ability to take rejection effortlessly was my most redeeming quality.

Even animals could sense something wasn't right with me, a being seemingly out of place. With heads tilted, their confusion appeared as indifference to me. It seemed apathy was a trait in our four-legged friends as well. Little did I know at that time that their awareness, or canine perception, was triggered for another reason.

A Zero trying to fit in often leads to a deeper rejection. In my experience, I could see a physical or spiritual recoil. For this reason, I let the world be, just be. I found a measure of happiness in this approach to life, call it self-actualization.

Well, I guess I was fortunate that my family had money. Lots of it. I am the son of a brilliant inventor who saw a solution to every problem, present company excepted. Growing up, I helped with my dad's business and took on the role of a personal confidante for his new ideas. The relationship was all business, no familial bonding, rather a more accurate description would be a business-like senior to junior associate affiliation. Although I have always felt disconnected from the world, especially its sunnier side, ideas don't show indifference, only people can. What's the old dad joke? What's the difference between ignorance and indifference? I don't know and I really don't care. Regardless, we saw small ideas take shape, put into action, and grow into fantastic products. Small ideas became big. Bigger than we could ever have imagined. One invention involved robotics in medical technology; well, never mind, it doesn't seem important right now. It's more critical to find out where I am. Does my family know I'm missing? Would they even notice?

God help me as I silently scream in desperation once again. Fear consumes every inch of my body and soul to find out where I am. Questions and pleas repeat in my head in rapid fire with the familiar and confusing response returned. "Stay calm, Buddy Boy. Stay calm."

Still struggling in this cold and dark cocoon, my mind races. How can someone hear me if I can't speak? I search the darkness again but see nothing. It's the horror of a night terror from which I couldn't wakeup or scream for help. Silent pleas of deliverance alternate with thoughts of panic and dread. "Who are you, Dammit?! Where am I?! Please help me! It's so cold and dark here. Am I dead?" There can't be any other answer to this question, right? Was I condemned to hell for a life wasted? Was this voice the embodiment of a hellish torment and punishment, pretending to rescue me for eternity? But it wasn't the hell that I had envisioned during my childhood, no images of hellfire or the devil in a red suit with horns and a pitchfork ruling the underworld. I had fallen into the abyss, and yet it wanted me for some unknown purpose. Would I reside here in this hellish state, a sort of limbo, reliving all my pain, both past and present, until my destiny would be revealed?

I pleaded for an answer. "Please tell me what you want."

An evil laugh echoed across the abyss and over the melody

of murmurs that had continued unabated. "You." The laughter grew louder and more terrifying.

Me? What does that mean? What does the owner of this spectral voice want from me? It felt like someone, or something, was next to me now and within arm's reach. I had visions of a hawk circling me as its prey, as it continued to speak with a more slithery and ominous tone. Faster and faster, it flew around me, inching closer. The darkness surrounding me made the sounds and commotion nauseating. Flashes of an image came through the emptiness of the void, but it was only a shape, nothing more. My body quaked at hearing the voice's offer. "A choice, an alternative, for a new beginning." The corporeal and spiritual reality of the abyss came into focus. The Atlantic is a cold and dark place, especially underwater.

And so, the story of my life, death and rebirth begins.

CHAPTER 2

Let's start with my experiences with higher education. During my time in college, I had sleepwalked through a year of scholarly tedium. Wake up. Shower. School. Work. Home. My daily personal journey of lather, rinse and repeat. I only went there to make my father happy and as a dying wish from my mom, the most wonderful mother in the world. An angel from heaven who loved me without reservation, perhaps with rose colored glasses and a desire to shield me from the world's malevolent side. Little did I know, she protected me because she knew how evil the world could be and didn't want to see me lose an inner light that she said I had. Mom saw me as others didn't, but I lost her. Or should I say, we lost her. We were a relatively happy family but that all changed when cancer visited us during my high school years and death took her away. A dark cloud of bereavement blanketed our home for months. Afterall, my dad and kid sister, Yo-Yo, mourned her as well.

My sister was named Chiara at birth, which fit her soul perfectly as she was *a daughter of light*. We called her Yo-Yo because she knew how to bounce from the highs and lows of daily life. She shared a glow that only my mom and she had. My sister had a knack for drawing and painting. A couple years ago, she won an award for her painting of an angel enveloping my mother as she was succumbing to the hell of her disease. If I only saw what she saw. She was a warrior. The judges at the art contest called her painting "enlightened and showed the work of an artist beyond her years." Now that's a compliment.

My mom was perfect. Born on Leap Day and at a time when young people still had hope for a better world, Mom had a Native American soul whose spirit and family history spanned across centuries. I had always heard that Leap Day was a special day that carried a deep spiritual meaning. Since both Mom and Yo-Yo were both born on a Leap Day and shared a special bond, Mom would always remind me to put an extra candle on the cake every four years. While I wasn't born in a leap year, I similarly had a special bond with both. It was the sort of spiritual and mental connection that I could never describe adequately. Mom and Yo-Yo could sense my pain, both physical and emotional, and were ready to help me remedy it at a moment's notice.

Mom was also a delight to all the senses. She loved to cook. Breakfast was her specialty, as if she invented the omelet. No skinny little things, rather they were fluffy cakes, seemingly pulled from the clouds, absolute comfort food. A savory aroma of cinnamon rolls permeated the house and left all of us salivating for hours. The sight of her eased the minds and souls of everyone she met. Mom could calm a person in torment and a soul battered by the world, simply with a soft smile or a reassuring touch. When she spoke, it was never harsh and or unkind. Her voice had a melody that only Mozart could have created. When I lost her, I lost part of my own essence. It was like losing an arm or a leg; the phantom wounds would be a constant reminder even when healed. Mom, where are you? You loved me too much. I wasn't ready for what was to come. The bad men aren't coming…I think they're already here.

My parents met while growing up in a place where the Southwest met the Great Plains. My dad's family, the Evermores, lived close to a Native American reservation that dated back to the late 1800s, and the family developed a lasting bond with members of the local tribe. They became friends for life, through good times and bad. My dad, Constantine Evermore Jr, was named for his father, and was the quiet one while my mom was the warrior, just like Yo-Yo. Mom would often call my dad JR, especially when she was upset with him. He always felt at ease when she was near him, even though she had a knack for finishing his sentences and getting him to do things that made him uncomfortable, like being social or greeting people with a smile. I could only imagine how he would have turned out if he had never married my mom, probably as socially awkward as me.

The Evermores were ranchers although Dad didn't develop a fondness for the outdoor life. My grandfather was known to help his many friends any time they needed assistance. Whether it was repairing a truck, breaking in a mustang, or building a shed, he became known as the local Mr. Fix It. Favors were given without request for recompense and were often returned twofold. The locals would tell me tall tales about my grandfather during my school vacation visits each summer. My favorite two stories about him were his killing of a rampaging bear with one shot when he was a teenager and his attempt to win my grandmother's heart. Both stories showed the type of man he was, strong and sensitive. We called him Grandfather out of respect; the name fit him perfectly.

While he could tangle with a bear, my grandmother was another matter. Grammie, as we called her, was unconquerable and took delight in torturing the boy she loved. He had tried for months to convince her for a date, but all of his attempts ended with him falling figuratively flat on his face. Something about her made him weak in the knees. Grammie told me that the best the things in life worth winning take effort. She was right. Grandfather treated her like a queen for his entire life. Nothing less would do.

During one of summer visits to the ranch, Grammie told me

about the day she finally stopped tormenting the man who would become the love of her life and agreed to a date. Her description of that day was so beautiful that she made me believe there was hope for me, although this thought would ultimately be the first casualty of meaningless life of a zero.

Grandfather had been away for the afternoon attending to ranch business in town and Grammie had noticed my nervous energy while he was away. I frantically paced the floor and periodically gazed out the window to see if Grandfather's truck was coming up the driveway.

"Jo-Jo, you are one jittery jack rabbit today. Even the dogs are puzzled at your shenanigans." Grammie placed her hands on shoulders and whispered in my ear, "No matter how long he's away, I miss him terribly too. What do you say if we go wait for your grandfather on the porch and drink some fresh lemonade?" She walked toward a kitchen counter to grab the lemonade pitcher and two glasses full of melting ice.

"That's a great idea." I loved my grandmother's lemonade. Its sweetness was only surpassed by my grandmother's heart.

Grammie approached me an in true gentleman fashion, I asked to carry the tray because that's what my grandfather would do. "Please, Grammie, let me carry that out."

She gazed at me with her eyebrows raised and smiled

gently. "Are you sure? It's a big tray."

"Yes, I can do it." I was barely 10 years old at the time but that didn't matter. My grandfather taught me to be a gentleman, to hold doors open for others, to treat others with respect, and most of all, to be attentive to Grammie, Mom and Yo-Yo. Chivalry wasn't dead in Grandfather's eyes.

We made our way to the porch and to the old rocking chairs that looked like they were made a hundred years ago. I placed the pitcher of lemonade on a small table that was situated between the chairs. The lemonade was a welcome treat since it was an excessively hot July day. Sitting on the chairs and slowly rocking back and forth, Grammie looked across the ranch with a contemplative gaze. She always took delight in the serenity produced by the quiet and leisurely moments on the ranch. This moment would be special for me too. "Jo-Jo, did you ever hear about my first date with your grandfather?"

"No, I haven't. Did he take you to the movies or for ice cream?" I was always excited to hear any story about this great man, even if it was about a date.

"Not quite. The rodeo was in town for the annual 4th of July celebration, so I was expecting him to take me there. But he surprised me. We went to a clearing on the edge of a hill on the far side of town. He had a picnic blanket and basket all set up for us already. For the next two hours, your grandfather looked at me and smiled as I rambled on endlessly about silly and unimportant topics. I was nervous for the first time in my life. My brain and mouth were out of control, operating non-stop at about 100 miles an hour. Finally, I asked him to say something. 'Why won't you say anything? You're just sitting back, smiling at me like a mischievous little devil.'

He was leaning back on one elbow and continued to smile. He tells me, 'You are most the beautiful person in the whole world. I love watching and hearing you talk.' Can you believe he said that. He always been a rascal."

"That sounds like Grandfather."

"Yes, it does. Then as if on cue, the 4th of July fireworks exploded and filled the sky. I couldn't believe that a man with a reputation of being a bear killer could be so sensitive. We had our first kiss that night against the backdrop of fireworks exploding overhead. I was smitten."

"Wow, you and Grandfather kissed. Yuck!"

"Jo-Jo, you know we were young once upon a time." Grammie erupted in laughter, and I laughed along with her. Glancing to the long driveway leading to the house, Grammie noticed Grandfather's truck approaching. "Well, it looks like he's back now."

Grandfather pulled up next to the house and walked up the front stairs. "What are you two doing? I can hear the laughter five miles away."

"Oh, CE, we're just having a little fun waiting for you."

"I'll bet." Bending over slightly, Grandfather gently kissed Grammie on the forehead. "Sorry, the meeting took longer than I expected, but it's all good now. Jo-Jo, let's go to the barn and get horses ready for our morning ride tomorrow. They could use a good brushing."

I jumped as soon as he said let's go. Nothing would stop me from being with him as much as I could. At that age, I didn't understand death yet.

While I was not great with horses, my fondest memories were our morning rides around the ranch. Grandfather would laugh when I awkwardly stumbled without fail trying to get on my horse, a beautiful palomino that he bought for me. His amusement, however, made me feel warm and loved, and not belittled. He had a way of filling me with confidence that I could meet any challenge head-on. He was the man I wanted to be.

Grammie's story reinforced my desire to be a man like my grandfather. I mimicked his every move, mannerism, and vocal intonation. We would walk through town and hear greetings from his many friends. They were good people. One of the best was

Sandy, the owner of the local ice cream shop. Sandy would say the same thing each time we dropped by, "Hey, CE. I see you brought your twin in again today. Two large double thick vanilla milk shakes for my best customers?" Grandfather smiled with pride when he looked at me. I felt 10 feet tall beside him. After our daily excursions of fishing or riding, my grandmother would laugh at seeing her "two men of the house".

I was devastated when death took my grandparents. Grammie had died suddenly, and he followed soon thereafter, heartbroken. Without question, their presence would have a profound impact on my life during my awkward teenage years. My aunt once told me that my grandfather talked about how much he loved our summers together. The sadness of their passing hit me hard. I don't think I ever recovered from this first tragedy.

The relationship between my dad and his parents was slightly more complex. Dad was always engrossed in his science and engineering books. So much so, he earned a scholarship to a world renown university in Boston. My grandparents never truly understood him, but they made sure he was nurtured and loved. Disconnected from the world around him, my dad wasn't generally receptive to their parental love.

In a lot of ways my dad and I were so similar, an amoeba splitting from its parent cell. His only respite from the daily tedium and snarky comments directed at him was my mom,

Marley. Apparently, her father liked Reggae music. Her favorite song was Three Little Birds. She would hum the tune whenever she felt happy, which was always. My maternal grandparents passed away before I was born. I wished they were here too. The stories Mom told me about them were captivating. They were the source of great spirit and strength that filled their daughter.

Mom and Dad would meet after school in an empty pasture and stare at the clouds. It was their own version of heaven on earth, where no worries existed and the noise from the world could be shut out. They were best friends, partners from the start.

One day, as they were walking home from the daily monotony that was high school, the neighborhood bullies – a group of four knuckleheads and fellow classmates - pounced on my dad with their usual taunts and abuse. They would never mess with my mom as I think the taunts were their misguided way of trying to impress her. She could easily ignore them, her way of dealing with bullies without the need for a fist fight. Sometimes, she would let them know how she felt about their childish taunts, causing them to back off. But that only deepened the pain in my dad, as his tormentors would ultimately hit back at his perceived need for a protector. Finally, after an afternoon of pounding beers and ditching classes, this group of knuckleheads crossed the line and made a crass comment to my mom. It's amazing how alcohol can fuel bravery. "Hey, look at the beautiful squaw! Why don't you come over here because I got a reservation for you?" An absolute terrible play on words that made my dad snap and deliver a single ferocious punch to the main instigator, who happened to be the strongest one, Billy Mannion. I had always heard that you should confront the strongest adversary when dealing with a group of bullies, as the rest will soon lose their fake courage. Billy fell back with a thud and was out cold. No one knew how strong my dad was. Growing up on a ranch toughens a boy up. "JR, what did you do?" screamed my mom. Hearing the crack of Billy's jaw and seeing their tough friend unconscious on the ground, the other boys froze in place and dared not move. Mom tended to Billy and helped him regain consciousness; Dad was lucky he didn't die.

The sheriff, Billy's uncle, wanted to lock my father up and throw away the key. But to do that, he would have had to admit his nephew was bested by the local book worm and with one punch. For a family that prided itself on the strength of its male members, this was unbearable. The bully became the bullied. "What's wrong with you boy!" Billy's dad, Ray, berated him later after the boy's buddies brought him home. He lived up to his nickname, Rayger, that day. Pounding his clenched fist to Billy's chest to emphasize his anger, he made his feelings clear. "You let a little flea, beat you with one punch. You disgust me. You're no Mannion. You better fix this or you'll be nothing. Mannions never lose, boy. Never!" Turning to his daughter, who was just approaching her teen years, "My little mighty mouse is stronger than you'll ever be." Billy had no response, other than to stand motionless, shoulders down and eyes wide open. I imagine he had the appearance of someone with PTSD. Waving his hands dismissively, Rayger didn't want to see Billy anymore that day. "Go on, get out of my sight."

Well, Billy never fixed it. Several years later, while Dad was in college in Boston, Billy was found hanging in his father's barn. He decided to end his life, after years of familial cruelty and self-abuse to his liver, first with beer, then with whiskey, when beer couldn't ease his pain. That day took a toll on Dad as he receded deeper and deeper into his protective shell. He always thought in some way it was his fault. He should have just walked away. Sometimes, however, there are things from which you can't just run, as I would learn personally in the most difficult way imaginable.

From that fateful day, one of several in my story, Mom and Dad worked though his emotions and guilt so that this would never happen again. "Violence feeds violence," Mom would say. While my grandfather approved of how his son handled the bully, my mom would tell him we have to be better than this. Once a short fuse is lit, it's difficult to extinguish safely and quickly. Mom told me this story years later when I was dealing with my own high school bullies as a way of understanding my dad better and providing a real-life lesson for me. I really didn't understand my mother's message until it was too late. I had the normal teenage reaction to her story, inattentive and dismissive. After all, it's not like she was my age once, right?

My mother ultimately went to Boston to be with my dad as he could not bear being away from her. They married after college and their love story continued. He completed his undergraduate and graduate degrees in only four years and obtained a position at a local biotech firm. Mom completed her degree at another local college and became immersed in history. How can you not be when you live in Boston?

Mom became a history teacher with a penchant for telling colorful stories of the underdogs and disenfranchised. No topic scared her. She was always willing to discuss a difficult subject but with the frame of mind of understanding differing perspectives, as that's the only way a person can learn and grow. At times when presented with a point of view that leaned toward hate, she would respond with her normal comforting gaze. She would ask, "what is the benefit to us and our relationships when we disagree with something so vehemently or heatedly it drives us to the darker edges of our being. We lose ourselves. We should never confuse passion with heat. We should be able to listen to each other and try to understand someone's views. Only then can we grow." I tried Mom; I tried, but the world is cruel and doesn't have any sympathy for you or your opinion.

Every year, she would entertain us with her version of the true story of Thanksgiving and Chief Massasoit, the great sachem of the Wampanoags. I felt connected and disconnected from the story at the same time. I tried to imagine being on both sides of the narrative and think of what was and wasn't true to me. My head would spin until I didn't want to hear the story anymore. I would tell her that I wasn't interested in a story from 400 years ago, or in which local schools had Native American mascots for their team. I know she wasn't trying to preach to me on the topic, rather she just wanted to engage with me and have me develop my own opinions. "To open both ears," as she would say. I was so lost, but I was more worried about the here and now! Being a teenaged idiot and thinking only of myself on that last Thanksgiving we shared, I said, releasing all my pent-up frustrations, "Everyone has a complaint. Blah, blah, blah. Time to flip the record." Saying that last piece, I knew it would resonate with Mom, having grown-up in the '80s.

I knew the point of her stories wasn't to complain but to understand where we have been and where we are going. Understanding the balance between the past, present, and future was a common theme in her stories to me, or lectures as I called them. I just didn't feel like it mattered.

Oh, how I wished I could listen to her now!

CHAPTER 3

I met Jenny while at Massachusetts Commonwealth University, a prominent school situated on a scenic campus that had an excellent science college, which was my primary interest. MCU was rooted in a Catholic foundation that would have made my mother happy, even though it really didn't matter to me. Mom was spiritual and always enjoyed the faith's social principles to serve the less fortunate. Perhaps I was one of her less fortunate beneficiaries during our time together.

It was easy for me to melt into the scenery, when considering the frenetic daily life of a university. I made a couple of friends, acquaintances more so than friends. We would exchange the daily pleasantries about dorm life and classes. We would eat lunch together in the main dining hall to discuss our class projects, the pains of our work-study jobs and quality of the cafeteria food we were eating. Subsisting on devil's food cake and diet soda became a primary part of our food pyramid.

Sometimes, we discussed doing something fun; however, the topic of our conversation would become more like an enigma that we rarely could find a solution. They were a group of kids, but like me, a little afraid of life. So, we stayed in our own swim lanes and avoided the unnecessary awkwardness of interaction with the outside world. Video games became a regular diversion to spend our free time that was not devoted to academics.

And then, there was Jenny. She was a goddess, a jaw dropper. The sun glistened off her golden hair, creating a halo that engulfed her and overwhelmed all others in her orbit. She bewitched me. Little did I know she would be the catalyst for my odd journey through a watery purgatory.

My college career had started a year later than normal, as I thought my life was to follow a different and undetermined path away from higher education. I made up ground quickly, because school was never a problem for me. People were the problem; books were not. My mom had passed the year following my high school graduation, just after Christmas, and I had wanted to be with her as much as I could. She seemed OK with my choice, because I think she knew these would be our last days together. Mom did, however, make me promise to go to college and ultimately make my own destiny, and not have it made for me. She often pleaded with me as she lay dying. "Jonah, please learn to love yourself and enjoy life. The world is waiting for you."

I always enjoyed meandering across the Quad in the center of campus, as it afforded me an opportunity to fulfill my daily craving to spy on the world and possibly feed off the energy and happiness of others. At times, my view of the world and its indifference overwhelmed me. I would stare at the roofs of the many gothic buildings circling campus and contemplate a jump into an eternal dirt nap. Would everyone's life be better? Would my pain end? A final and fatal conclusion was never reached, but my life was about to change.

On one exceedingly warm early Autumn morning on campus, I noticed Jenny, giggling with her friends and without a care in the world. Her blonde locks sparkled in the sun as they always did, easily rendering me with temporary blindness. I couldn't stop staring at her and the shiny halo of light engulfing her body. Walking in a trance-like state, I nearly stumbled over one of the million shrubs circling the campus. It was then she looked over to me and smiled. I quickly looked away, and then, like a complete idiot I walked into my science professor, Sister Alicia, a Sister of Charity who had gotten her doctorate and now taught the principles of anthropology to the dull minds of the university's student population. For some odd reason, I found her class to be a comforting place, a haven for a lost soul.

It was a complete wipeout. I stammered through an apology while trying to avoid eye contact with anyone around me. As I picked up our books from the pavement, Sister Alicia could only laugh, "Mr. Evermore, where's the fire? We may need to put a bell on you." Thank God she wasn't hurt.

Jenny's reaction was a combination of hilarity and disbelief; possibly because her phone wasn't ready to video the spectacle of my ineptitude. I felt naked for all the world to see. No! No! No! The silent cry went through my mind with the pitch of a screaming locomotive. If I could have only vanished into the background. Instant invisibility, my usual super-power wasn't working that day.

A few days later, Jenny and I bumped into each other. Let's put "bumped" in quotes for now. As I look back at that fateful day--yes, remember I have a few of these for you--I can't believe I didn't see that the whole meeting was staged. What a fool? It was a perfectly innocent start to a modern horror movie. Yo-Yo would have known, but not me.

In a cute voice and with her head tilted innocently to the side, she asked, "Hi. Aren't you Jo-Jo?" Red flag number one; only my family called me Jo-Jo. But she said it in way that melted my heart and knocked me off my axis.

What? Who? Why? Huh? Stammering through a response, "Y-Y-Yes, yes, I'm Jo-Jo. I mean Jonah." Thinking about her next comment, I was paralyzed by fear. She offered, "I heard you're a science wizard or something, and I was hoping you could help me," she said with a twinkle in her eye and a smile that's only seen in the best romantic movies. "I am struggling with my science elective, Principles of Geology. I can't get a D. You must be super busy, and I hate to ask, but can you find it in your heart to help me?"

"Um, sure. Glad to." From there on, the world changed for me.

"Great. Let's meet up tomorrow. How's 4 o'clock in the library sound?"

Looking at floor, I avoided eye contact with her as best as possible. "Sounds good. I'll meet you in the front courtyard."

Jenny leaned in and kissed me gently on the cheek. "You're a doll. See you later."

Wow! With Jenny's kiss, my face turned 10 different shades of red. I was literally knocked off my feet. Slightly dazed, I held my cheek for the entire walk back to the dorm, trying to preserve this new and strange feeling of exhilaration. The kiss was one of the best moments of my life and I didn't want it to end.

We met for our first study session the next day. Sitting in a far corner of the old library, we went through her class syllabus and the results of her recent examination. While I tried to concentrate on scholarly matters, Jenny would rather focus her attention on me. She sat next to me, leaning in close, and gently touching my arm causing me to continually lose focus on the tutorial. I concentrated with all my might on the principles of plate tectonics, explaining how earthquakes happen and volcanoes form. I rambled on with my lesson for what seemed to be an eternity. All the while, Jenny was smiling, causing me to spiral into near panic.

Jenny sensed my emotional state and tried to relax me. "Jo-Jo, I don't know how your brain retains all this knowledge. I wish I was half as smart as you."

I couldn't imagine Jenny feeling inferior in any way. "No, no, you're smart. This isn't an easy subject."

Jenny shook her head and squirmed in her chair seductively. "You're too nice. Your parents must be proud of you."

The atmosphere suddenly turned cold with the thought and memory of my mom. I sat back in my chair with a deep sigh. "Sorry, my mom passed away recently, and I still haven't gotten over it."

Jenny took notice of my sorrow and gently caressed my arm. "I'm so sorry. I didn't know. Seeing your reaction, she must have been a remarkable person."

Fixated on a comforting gaze of the most beautiful girl in

school, it was a moment I would never forget. "She was a pure spirit who loved everyone."

"Wow, that's awesome." In an instant, Jenny's mood changed. Staring into the distance, Jenny was clearly affected by our conversation. She sat motionless for a few seconds before telling of her own loss. "My dad died a few years ago too. He was the definition of the *World's Best Dad*." Her voice tailed off as she finished speaking, a clear sign of the effect her dad and his death had on her life. From this shared experience, a bond formed.

We spent the rest of our time in the library exchanging stories of the parents we lost. Losing track of time, we finally noticed we had been talking for hours and the library was closing for the night. We made plans to meet for lunch the next day, and I fell deeper into Jenny's Venus Flytrap's clutches.

Over the coming weeks, we grew closer with each passing day, evolving eventually into love, or so I thought. Lunch turned into dinner which then turned into movie dates and overnight delight. We began our affair, first as study partners then as soul mates, but the party was just beginning, and its ending was going to be a haymaker.

CHAPTER 4

If ignorance is bliss, then I must have been in heaven. Our time together was magical. I met new people and became part of the in-crowd. I went beyond my comfort zone, as small as it was. Prior to this, expanding my comfort zone would have been wearing socks that weren't white. Jenny made me feel alive and desirable. It was pure magic. I felt like a god. The kids on campus saw me differently now. They took notice of a boy that they wanted to know. My table in any one of the university dining halls would be full of people who wanted to be with me, even fawn over me, just because of my association with Jenny. I was suddenly cool, but my suspicious nature would often wonder whether I was holding court or was a mere court jester.

Every so often during these daily lunch sessions with new batch of friends, Sister Alicia would approach and ask if this was a good use of my time. It seemed Sister Alicia didn't care much for my new companions. If I had only seen what she saw, my path would have been easier, but more boring. Definitely, it would have been more uninteresting for sure.

Folding her arms, the benevolent nun shook her head. "Mr. Evermore, perhaps you can exert the same level of effort and enthusiasm in class before your brain goes completely dry."

The boisterous mood at the table suddenly dropped to a completely subdued level. All of us stared at her in a sort of frozen and speechless panic that's normally associated with a child being scolded by a parent. Seeing her disappointment in me, I slumped back into my chair, regretting the distress I caused. As odd as it sounds, her opinion did matter to me, I responded with a sheepish, "Sorry."

Sister stood close to me and folded her arms for added emphasis. "Please don't apologize to me. Expressing sorrow provides momentary relief from our transgressions. Sincerity lies with the truth that we learn from our experiences and in changing for the better. Find your path, Mr. Evermore. Find your path, young man." She had a way of sounding almost pleasant when cutting someone down to size.

As Sister Alicia walked away, Jenny turned to the group and immediately sought to belittle her. "Geez. Thanks Professor Penguin, didn't know we needed a new life coach." The table erupted in laughter. I joined in, somewhat half-heartedly, but I could see Sister Alicia's head shaking as she walked away in the distance. Maybe the world is better than I thought. No dice!

As I recall that day, sitting at the table with my new crew and enjoying a laugh at another's expense, my thoughts wander again and turn back to the abyss.

Why am I so cold? I still can't see anything. I hear the suffocating sound of water again. The dark abyss continues to call me, beckoning me faintly to some purpose, or fate, that I can't yet understand. What was the choice being offered to me? "Be calm, Buddy Boy, be calm. Join us. Join us." Join whom? Wake up. Wake up. Where am I? Somebody, please find me. Is it only a dream or is this what death feels like? How would I know? I've never been dead before. A fever of panic and dread engulfs me again.

I took to being a member of the in-crowd like a fly takes to dog waste. Walking across campus, I basked in the glow and popularity of my attachment to Jenny, or Slim, as I affectionately called her. Being a lover of old movies – especially those old film noir and gangster movies – I eventually became comfortable enough to give her a nickname. If it was good enough for Bacall, then it was good enough for Jenny. What a lucky bastard! How did you snag that prize? You're punching above your weight class, kid. I quietly celebrated my fortune as divine providence, but not anymore.

Parties every weekend. When there wasn't a party, we

made our own, together. I fell hard and fast. Little did I know it was all part of the setup, a great con game. Her touch was equally exhilarating and comforting. I can remember those times when she convinced me to go dancing. Me, dancing? One night, we grooved the night away dancing to classic '80s music at the University Pub along with other members of my young generation who had developed a love for the decade's music. I was totally lost, yet I thought I was found. How was that possible? The punchline is coming and folks it's going to hit hard.

Our party mates were Jenny's friends, who looked like they were pulled off a catwalk – not a single blemish or physical imperfection on any of them. They were ugly in other ways. How could I have overlooked their ugliness when they belittled other people who weren't part of the Beauty Crew – the BCs as they called themselves? I was too immersed in all things Jenny to adequately dissect Chip, Barclay, TT, T-Rex, Bella and the rest of the merry bunch of miscreants. Here's the rundown. Chip was the preppy model with a penchant for demeaning everyone and anyone that wasn't at his level, socially or physically. Barclay was his girlfriend and was more interested in staring at herself in the mirror than connecting with people. T-Rex was the muscle who was allowed into the group due to the size of his, well let's say his wallet. Bella was untouchable, so she thought, as she thought herself the next Princess Grace. TT was somewhat normal in comparison to the others, but she found T-Rex irresistible for some odd reason. Maybe it was a lack of self-respect or self-confidence.

The BCs would sit and crowd watch students walking by them in the dining halls. They could find the smallest flaw and exploit it, usually to their benefit. The two more common benefits were getting others to prop up their grades or find them a new place to party. Their effortless and confident manner presented an attraction for me, like a moth to a flame. If I had watched the BCs more closely and had not been enchanted by their glamour, I would have seen their true ugliness. I became one of the gilded youths, of little worth and substance. The lies, sarcasm, and perverse sense of humor were all there. Be assured, their day will be coming.

I am beginning to wake-up. It's still cold. It's still dark. Mom, are you there?

CHAPTER 5

My mom had factored into my life in so many ways, including influencing a fondness for old movies at a very young age. None of those silly Cowboy and Indian movies. Rather classic film noir and gangster movies that were so unique and stylish that sometimes I would fantasize I was that hero or anti-hero who ate up scenery with one stare. I dreamed of being a man so confident that women would fall into my arms like rain drops. After my grandfather, Bogie and Cagney were my heroes. Tough as nails but sensitive when they needed to be. I wanted to be like them but didn't know how to do it. It was beyond my reach. As odd as it sounds for a child of the 21st century, there's something about the purity and simplicity of the drama and tone of those movies that took hold of me. The stories always felt timeless to me. Conflicted souls, alienated from the world, seemingly headed down a dark path involuntarily but being brought to the light by good people, usually by someone who loved him without condition. I yearned for that from the outside world.

We would frequent the local theater that showed old movies for a new generation and in the way they should be seen, on the big screen. One Saturday, we watched a beautiful but corny Rock Hudson and Doris Day comedy classic from the '50s that had no resemblance to reality, a far cry from the film noir movies I loved. We laughed throughout the movie, understanding that this was our escape from the real world for two hours. We enjoyed our day and never overthought the silliness of every scene. My mom would tell me to enjoy life, and for those two hours, I would.

We would often go to lunch at Giuseppe's Kitchen for our favorite Saturday afternoon indulgence, a large double dough pepperoni pizza. It was ambrosia for the body and soul. As we ate, Mom would weave in small talk with a continuation of our pep talks. "What did you think of the movie today? Wasn't it funny?"

Chewing on a slice of pizza, I mumbled a half-hearted and snarky agreement. "Yup, except for all the unbelievable stuff, it was good, but I think the movie actually gave me cavity from all artificial sweetness in it."

Mom leaned back in her chaired and laughed at my response. "Jo-Jo, c'mon. You have got to be kidding me. I saw you laughing. At one point, I thought you were going spill your bag of popcorn all over the theater's floor."

"Well, maybe a few times." I was caught with my hand in the proverbial cookie jar. I did like the movie.

"Didn't you think the main characters had such confidence in themselves, but they first had to learn to see the world and its beauty."

It was easy for mom to transition to a pep talk and connect the movie to me. She could turn any conversation on a dime. "Don't let the beast in? The wolf will be your guide. You control your destiny. Please try to love and believe in yourself! Our path in life is not predetermined or inescapable, unless we make it so through our own action or inaction." My mom's favorite saying was "Don't let life happen to you. Live it!"

"Mom, OK, can I finish my lunch now?"

Mom looked at me oddly as we finished lunch. There was a sadness in her eyes that I had never seen. I sensed she was holding back telling me something. Like any normal teenager, I thought it was about being disappointed in me for not following her life lessons. Days later, I would find out she wanted to tell me about her cancer diagnosis, but she didn't have the emotional strength that day to upset her precious son. Mom, I'm so sorry for not seeing things clearly. You were always a great teacher to a bad student who didn't listen well.

I never understood what she meant about the beast or making my own future. Afterall, how does a teenager see his future when he's still trying to figure out puberty? And I never really paid attention to her message about the wolf, other than it had some spiritual meaning. Maybe I should have fed it, or at least googled it. Later, I would discover the meaning of her message and understand the divine battle within all of us for our souls.

Dad, on the other hand, was always distant. He never liked to hug us. I guess he didn't know how, which was odd considering how nurturing his parents were. Maybe, it was an unresolved issue or unintended outcome of the Billy Mannion tragedy. He grew more distant after my mom died. This wasn't surprising as she was his center, his foundation. As dad's business – Evermore Ideas – grew from one invention to many, we enjoyed a comfortable life. One of our shared interests was fixing old cars. When I was in grade school, I would watch him for hours on Sundays restoring an old beauty from the '50s or 60s. He taught me all about the engineering that went into these beautiful machines. I soaked in the knowledge with joy, thinking I had found a purpose in my life.

For a time, I was happy, but as soon as my dad finished a car, he would sell it. In his mind, if there's nothing left to fix then there was no purpose in keeping it. He couldn't find happiness in just enjoying the fruits of his, and our, labor. He always needed to find another car to restore. Perhaps the next car would be the one where he could find a level of joy or satisfaction. He never found it. I learned that happiness was a short-lived illusion and it's best to accept it. Dad's way of chasing happiness, unattainable as it was, was comparable to a child contorting his body and reaching for the brass ring on an amusement park ride. He needed to keep dreaming and inventing new gadgets and gizmos, but his brass ring would remain elusive.

My sister and I, on the other hand, were best buddies. Since the local elementary and high schools were on the same route home, we would walk home together. She would tell me about her day. Her perspectives were often beyond her years. Yo-Yo would pick interesting topics like the day we discussed her issue with the English language.

Meandering our way home one sunny afternoon, I decided to have a little fun. "Why do you think English is so difficult?"

Stopping for a moment and appearing dumbfounded at my question, Yo-Yo responded with typical youthful frustration. "Really, have you paid attention at all during vocabulary lessons? Seriously, Jo-Jo?"

"Apparently not," I said with a slight snicker. As we continued our walk, I knew Yo-Yo was going to continue with her comedic rant.

"Look at some words that are just nuts," she said while hopscotching her way home. "Wind or wind? While the wind was blowing outside, you had to wind the clock? Crazy, crazy, crazy. Let's talk about lead, lead, or led? A new teacher will lead the class tomorrow and talk about the dangers of lead in our drinking water. Yesterday, she led the class about the dangers of lead.

Here's another one. Have you read Red, my favorite book about colors? Why is slaughter pronounced differently than laughter? Do I need to keep on going? My little brain begins to hurt every time I think about it. Let's talk about danger and manger. Take out the *d* and *m*, you have anger, which is the feeling that English vocabulary is causing in me." Quickly changing the subject as she can do so well, "Boy, am I hungry too!"

As always, she had a point. "Yo-Yo, where did you learn about the word slaughter?" I had to ask, since that is a strong word for someone in elementary school.

"It was about some Cowboy and Indian thing that happened like a gazillion years ago. I really didn't pay much attention to the story. I can think of more words." She repeated her grievance against the English language as she continued to play pretend hopscotch for the duration of our trip home. "I think the President should make me queen of the English language so that I can fix all the weird words and create new ones. All the new ones will be happy words that make you think about puppies and flowers."

Yo-Yo never ceased to amaze me but I'm not sure how the President could make her a queen of the English language. That innocence she had was precious to me and my family. Listening to her daily musings rose my spirits tenfold. She could do no wrong.

Our conversations would be something I would always cherish.

On days we could not walk together, Yo-Yo would wait for me to come home. On those days, she would have me pose for a painting and always saw something different in me. It's like she could see all the pain and suffering I experienced daily yet was able to see something good trying to reveal itself. She saw through my outer shell, my defensive ring, and painted images that were both shadow and light. My eyes seemingly hollowed by the world, yet a tiny ember visible and waiting for a spark.

On one occasion, a few years after debating her grievance with the English language, I wanted to know more. "Why do you paint me like this? Do you really see me this way, sad and lost?" My questions were hanging at the tip of my tongue like a pinata waiting to be crushed. Her response was always the same.

"I see you, my sad and goofy brother. You're perfect. You're a little lost; you just need to find out who you really are." Really! What did she mean? What did she see? Yo-Yo was too smart for me to understand what she meant, or was it I didn't want to understand her, because it would be a validation of my place in the world. Calling me "lost" hit me hard.

Yo-Yo loved me unconditionally and always made me promise to never leave her when it was time for college. I always did. I even agreed to stay close to home for college as it made dad and her happy. For as distant as my father was, I knew he loved us deep down even though he couldn't show it. He was a good man but that distance between us remained as expansive as the Grand Canyon when I left for college. He was busy working 12-hour days with little family time, except for our Sunday car restoration sessions or when my mom could get out of the house for a family dinner. I get it. He tried his best to provide a good life for us. If he only knew that I needed him more than a McMansion in the suburbs. He parented the way he thought best, disconnected from the kids yet present in physical form when he was needed. I wonder if he ever saw how things could have been different beyond his Robo-dad approach. Lather, rinse, repeat. For all the emotional support we needed, there was my mother, my rock.

CHAPTER 6

One evening, before that fateful day when I met Jenny, dad rang my mobile phone. During that conversation, I felt the need, an urge to ask if he missed Mom. It was building inside of me for quite a while. I knew how detached emotionally he could be, but Yo-Yo and I needed more from him. On the day of the funeral, he just stared blankly as the workers lowered my mother's body into her grave. It was too robotic for me. Where was the emotion? After a moment of silence, he growled at me. "Absolutely. What kind of question is that? I miss her terribly." His passion was evident before his voice tailed off; I imagined him gazing into the distance as he often did.

"Sorry Dad, sometimes I just need you to tell or show me."

"I know, son, it's been difficult for all of us. I'm sorry I snapped at you."

"That's OK dad. I understand." He was always great provider but that bond between us could have been tied more tightly. Knowing how he felt about Mom partly reassured my concerns about dad's feelings.

The question also needed to be asked, because I heard that he had been growing closer to his secretary, Kathy, Karen or something. I had never met her but apparently, she was beautiful, stunning was the word used to describe her. This was the same secretary that would send home care packages when my mom was sick, mostly my mom's favorite desert, cheesecake. Mom loved cheesecake. We couldn't understand why, but she loved it.

It seemed the two of them grew closer as both were widowed and provided a level of comfort that both needed. Dad wanted to bring her over for dinner during Christmas break. But I wouldn't stand for it. No way! Never!

Dad dropped the topic for a few weeks, once he saw the tears well up in Yo-Yo's eyes. How can you hurt an angel? He couldn't; it wasn't in his nature. He was a good man affected by the world around him and his own demons of self-worth, traits he shared with me. My pain was growing, but Jenny was there for relief.

Mom! Where are you? I'm so cold. It's dark here.

As May approached, Jenny and I continued to grow closer together. She made me feel like I was the most important person in the world. We were completely in sync. We fit together like pieces of a puzzle, physically and spiritually. It was only natural that Jenny set up a date to introduce me to her family – a twin brother, a close male cousin and her mom. I don't know why she never told me she had a twin, but I would soon come to know the boys as two parts of the Trinity of Evil, mocking everything that was good in the world. Jenny's mom would be at the top of that pyramid. In Jenny, I felt more disappointment than anger, odd to say but true.

They recommended a day of boating. Her brother, Decker, and cousin, Riley, enjoyed taking weekend trips out of Gloucester harbor to enjoy the solitude of the Atlantic, do some fishing and drink some beer on their boat, a beautiful 35-footer that was recently restored. They developed a love of boating from their dad, although I understand this was a more recent acquisition. Life is good, I guess.

On that warm May morning, I met Jenny at the local diner that was off campus for a surprise. As I rolled up in my old '69 Chevelle, a car I began restoring a few years ago with the help of my dad and in-between our private business sessions, I saw Jenny waiting patiently for me. "Hey Slim. What's the surprise today," I asked. With excitement, Jenny told me that she arranged for us to spend the day with her brothers and mother on her family's boat; however, she asked that we keep our day a secret so that we could have a day with her family without interruption. It seemed to be a great way for us to get to know each other.

Her brother and cousin picked us up at the diner parking lot because the boatyard had limited parking. She didn't want our day spoiled by the incessant phone calls from friends and family, which was odd since we were going to be with her family. Not capable at saying no to her, I agreed and said nothing further.

The boys started calling me guppy during the car ride due to my lack of seafaring experience. Jenny had warned them that I didn't care much for boating. She gave the boys a nice opening to have fun at my expense. Decker was especially blunt in mocking me, "Hey guppy, we've got a couple buckets for you when you get sick. Would you like to wear a life vest too? I think we have one in a kid size."

Waving my hands in response, I mustered up as much bravado as possible, "No problem here, life vests are for babies."

"Good to hear. Good to hear." Riley responded quickly, but this time with a menacing tone that bewildered me. What did he mean? Did I miss the joke?

Once we got to the boat, there was the continued banter from the boys who were already primed to harass the kid who was dating the family jewel. Even though it was early in the day, the boys had the smell of beer on their breath. I took it in stride as Jenny would tell them to stop if she felt the teasing was going too far. Her mom was nice enough, greeting me with the requisite pleasantries. "Hi, I'm Kat. So nice to finally meet the boy who captured my Jenny's heart. Hope you're ready for a day on the ocean?" At the time, I should have noticed how cold she sounded when she introduced herself to me. Connecting the dots now, I have a fantastic super-power, hindsight, and it's perfect.

All was going well, until that is, we got to an anchorage spot, out near the Stellwagen Bank. That's when Jenny's mom came from below deck with a cold look in her eyes. Nervously, I asked if anything was wrong? Was there a problem with the boat? The boat rocked in the waves, up, down and side to side, adding to the instability of the situation.

It was then she began to tell me the story of a little girl who found her brother hanging in a barn many years ago. "Guppy," she spoke with a tone that could freeze water, "can you imagine a young girl finding her brother's lifeless body hanging in the barn? His skin already turning blue, we imagined he must have been hanging there for hours, alone. Can you conceive the emotional and spiritual impact this would have on a child seeing someone she loved ending his life? His suicide hit me hard. At first, I was overcome with sadness and depression, sleeping long hours and avoiding contact with others. I was devastated."

Kat paused a moment to wipe a tear from her eye before continuing her story. "Devastated, until a rage came alive inside of me. My blood boiled. Do you know how death can cause a deep imprint and hole in your soul? One that doesn't heal easily. And the only way to heal is to take blood for blood, vengeance pure and simple. The person who drove my brother to do this had to pay."

Kat turned her attention to the far horizon. "Well, that's the way I learned it. Teaching me the true meaning of life, my father showed me that the meek do not inherit the earth. He would tell me, 'Alpha dogs ruled. Betas and sheep followed or got chewed up.' My father could be a hard man to love but easy to respect. He was a pure Alpha dog. Gone but never forgotten, he wasn't called "Rayger" because of his cheery personality. I was his Mighty Mouse and he made sure I knew it. Any feelings I entertained that he was also responsible for my brother's suicide were quickly changed with his frequent lessons. I am my father's daughter." Kat slapped her hands together with ferocity and repeatedly, indicating how he drilled this into his pupil.

Aware of my family's story, I was stunned at hearing her father's nickname. A sense of impending doom filled the air, so thick it felt like it could suffocate me.

Pausing a moment to enjoy the look of my fear on my face, Kat continued her story. "It's been a long and hard road getting us to this point. Let me tell you the rest. I got married at 18 to a man, John Casey, who would bring me to Boston, and closer to my desire for revenge. Growing to love my husband and with the birth of our twins, we raised a happy family. It was the best time of my life. I guess I was lucky to have had him for 16 years before the angel of death came for him and resuscitated the sleeping Alpha-dog in me. So much so, I didn't feel the need to be the Alpha-dog any longer. Eventually, I was able to find work as a secretary locally to support my family. Then, one day I heard that a brilliant inventor needed a new administrative assistant to keep his work organized. What luck! Let's just say he was dazzled by me, much in the way Jenny overwhelmed you. "

Jenny trembled and pleaded with her mother. "Mom, please."

Kat waved her off dismissively. "But don't worry there was no funny business. He loved his wife too much to fully fall for my charms. It was all business. When I saw how happy your family was and that your mom was dying, my plan became easier to achieve. Mannions never lose."

Panic and shock consumed me as my voice trembled. "What did you say? Did you say Mannions never lose? How do you know that name?"

Kat's satisfaction was evident as she stood in a superhero pose in front of me, hands on her hip, back straight and chin up. "Now do you know who I am? Your mother must have told you the story of our families."

The boys circled me, shouting various taunts and threats. With each pass, they would repeatedly throw bait at me to emphasize my position as their catch of the day. They were in a state of ecstasy, circling closer and closer to me like lions ready to pounce. Jenny stood to the side, emotionless and not partaking in the boys' games. I wasn't sure what she was doing or why didn't help.

Kat stepped closer to me to accentuate the ending of her story. "Guppy, I will marry your father and bleed him dry, emotionally, and financially. He paid for this boat after all with some fancy and undetected book-keeping on my part. He and your precious sister will have long and tormented lives. I will see to it. I took care of your mother. Fortune smiled on me when I heard of her illness. I knew she loved cheesecake and you guys didn't. Those little, single serving cheesecakes hid a perfectly undetectable secret that worked so well with her cancer. We couldn't risk Marley beating her illness, after all, terminal or not. Now, we need to deal with you since you've been preventing JR and me getting together. You've been such a nuisance. Your dad will mourn you and I will be there to gather the pieces. Billy, this is for you, brother."

I stared at her, motionless, frozen in time, as she finished her story. I became rattled at hearing the ensuing laughter all around me. Just then, one of the boys walloped me from behind sending me into the water, plunging slowly into its cold depths.

Descending, whispers from the dark filled my head, "The

beast has him now; we must wait. He should have been better prepared but there is hope for the wolf. We must wait. We have no choice but to wait." This seminal battle for my soul and fate between these opposing forces, natural enemies within the Trinity, kicked into full gear. The winner would be chosen by me, but would I be strong enough to make the right choice?

CHAPTER 7

I could see the boys and Jenny looking intently overboard at me as I slowly descended toward the ocean's bottom. It felt like an eternity as I struggled to breathe in a half-conscious state, before succumbing to a watery fate. I soon heard a mysterious voice calling me to be calm, asking me how I felt being betrayed by that girl. "Wouldn't it be nice if you had the chance to return the favor," the voice asked. "It wasn't your fault that this happened to you. The world did this to you. The world has always been against you, waiting for its moment to get rid of you." The voice wouldn't stop. "Do you know where you are now?"

More voices chimed in, "Join us. Join us." I could feel the ice-cold water surrounding me. I could taste salt. Mom, where are you?

With a slithering snake-like tone, an evil voice whispered, "Don't ask for your mommy, Buddy Boy. Toughen up and grow a backbone. Here is your choice. Do you want vengeance, or do you want to be a decaying guppy at the bottom of the ocean? Do you want to protect your sister? This is your destiny. Reach out and grab my hand."

Clasping onto the medal of St. Michael that hung around my neck, I wondered whether the voice was real or imagined. My mom gave me the medal at my confirmation years earlier as protection against evil. Well, that didn't work. I never removed the medal as it always gave me comfort as a spiritual connection to my mom, not that I believed greatly in its protective capabilities. My mind, as confused as it was, told me to fight and to not surrender to the voice.

Aren't I supposed to see some sort of light or dead ancestor? Am I really dead? Is this what purgatory feels like? Fight, that's all that made sense to me.

The voice continued whispering to me, singing a melody of discord until it reached an operatic crescendo. Trying to get me to acknowledge Jenny's betrayal while building my anger toward revenge, the voice overpowered my senses with periodic flashes of images of a gloating Kat and the boys along with intermittent images of my family in despair. These images were followed by long stretches of total darkness and continued to take their toll on me. It was, however, odd that Jenny wasn't in any of these images. "Forget the stupid medal. Join us." Those voices dripped with evil intent.

I fought for as long as I could, but the voice knew how to get through to me. As the expression goes, he played me like a fiddle. After what felt like an eternity had passed, I finally surrendered and made my choice, and reached out for a hand in the darkness. Saying yes changed my fate and faith. Going forward, vengeance became my creed, my religion. Almost immediately, I was scooped-up by a fishing net.

The net was from a Gloucester fishing trawler that was spending the day looking to fulfill its daily catch. Emptied onto the deck of the Fisherlady, I was dumped along with the other treasures of the sea. Did you know I hate seafood? But how could I be alive, I thought, my mind racing through all the possibilities. As I rose from the deck, I could feel the crew staring at me, not with wonder but with a complete lack of concern, as if they were expecting me. Some appeared to be scowling at me, possibly for ruining their day. There was a dog on deck as well, watching me intently. She was a beautiful black German Shepherd, but still a scary sight to behold for those unfamiliar with the breed. While animals had always seemed to hold an indifferent attitude toward me, this dog was different. Almost immediately, she came up to me and began licking my hand, crying with delight.

As I looked around the deck, shivering from the cold water that had soaked deeply into my bones, I tried to understand the difference in the weather. When I went into the water, it had been a sunny and warm day. When I came out it was cooler, cloudier and damper. And why weren't the men around me wearing summer clothes? I held on tightly to the St. Michael medal that was still wrapped around my neck. The net didn't dislodge the only source of comfort for me.

Escorted inside by a couple members of the crew, I caught a quick glimpse of the month on a calendar hanging on the wall. It was September. How can this be, surviving three or four months under water was not possible? I realized I had taken a fateful bargain during my time in a watery grave, but there was still no answer to what or who I was. A feeling of dread hit me, eyes darting side to side, and quietly hyperventilating at the thought of losing four months of time. Feeding my fright, the crew never spoke a word to me. They just stared at me, expressionless.

It was at that point; the boat's Captain came up and greeted me in a foreign language. It sounded like Spanish or Portuguese. Sitting on a bunk with a blanket draped around me, I struggled to understand him. High school foreign language class didn't prepare me for this.

Captain took note of my confusion. "Sorry, where are my brains? Sometimes, I forget what language I'm speaking. I see you've made a friend in Tres. Are you OK? It seems you've had quite an adventure," speaking now in flawless English. "What is your name, my friend?" I remained confused and tried to form words, but my lips and brain did not seem to be connected.

After a slight pause, the interrogation continued, "Can we call anyone? My name is Captain Joao; my friends call me Jo-Jo." What kind of coincidence or joke is this? We have the same nickname. Have I fallen into an alternate universe? I refuse to call him Jo-Jo.

I began to speak my name but then I thought it better to be safe. After all, who were these guys? I can't trust anyone. They could be working with the Mannions; here to torture me and finish me off. Thinking quickly, "My name is Isaac, Isaac Michael Noone." It was the name of my online alter ego I made up years earlier.

Captain put his hand on my shoulder to emphasize his compassion. "Isaac, such a strong name. Can I call your family?"

Recoiling from his touch and clenching my arms closely to my body trying to generate warmth, I shivered a response. "I have no family."

Captain's reply sounded more like a statement than a question at first. "Can you imagine a person ending up in my fishing net? I mean how did you end up in my net?"

My brain raced frantically for a response. Grasping for an incredulous reason, I whispered, "Just out for a boat trip for a few days by myself and my boat sank."

Captain inched closer to me as if he was a cheetah ready to pounce. "Where are you from? Did you send out an SOS?"

Still struggling to speak, I muttered a response. "Down south. I had no time for an SOS. It happened suddenly. Thanks for saving me."

"Down south? My favorite place. Let's get you warmed up and back on dry land. And it looks like you need a shirt. You must be freezing. Geez, those pants barely fit you too. We'll get you back to shore soon. I'm sure there are things you need to do when you get back."

"What do you mean?" I then stared at my hands and body, not recognizing what I saw. My body seemed different. But how?

"A young man like you must have something or somebody waiting for him." Captain's voice had an ominous tone now. Who was this guy?

Reacting angrily, "No, I said I have nobody!"

The boat continued its slow trip back the dock. During that time, I sat and wondered what was going to happen next when we reached dry land.

CHAPTER 8

As the boat pulled up to the dock, the crew stared at me oddly and was no longer expressionless. Inching closer and closer to me, they were like dogs putting up their noses to sniff the aroma of a freshly cooked steak, eyes wide open and staring at the source of that wonderful bouquet.

"Can you smell the power?" One by one, the crew began to whisper, echoing throughout the deck.

I looked back at them with apprehension and confusion. They gave me the creeps. If you looked up creepy in the dictionary, you would see a picture of the crew.

Tres growled at the crew, beckoning them to back off, which made me feel wanted and protected by a dog for the first time in my life. It felt great. Captain quickly shouted, "Enough guys. Don't try to scare our guest. Mr. Noone, or can I call you Isaac, do you have a place to stay in town?"

I maintained a safe distance from the crew. There was something unnatural about them, but I couldn't identify it. "No, the boat was my home."

Captain patted my back to reassure me. "Well, you can stay with me until you get back on your path."

My path? For some odd reason, I felt the need to go with him, his voice providing comfort and direction. "Sure, that'll be great."

I recognized the boat yard as the one where I left on the fateful trip with Jenny and her family. It was an odd feeling seeing the place where my journey began. It was more surreal than real. Things seemed different but I couldn't really pinpoint the change. My eyes wandered around the boat yard in confusion.

My new friend tapped my arm. "Hey, Isaac, are you alright?"

"Yes, Captain, I am." I refused to call him Jo-Jo.

We loaded up his truck and drove to his home. As I passed the sights in town that I knew so well, I noticed more differences, stores damaged and boarded up, names of businesses changed, exteriors painted new colors, and a car model I had never seen before. Then came a shock to my sanity. It was a billboard advertisement for this year's new car, the brand-new electric

Mustang. An electric Mustang for 2022? Wait, what year was it? I've been gone for three years, not a few months. How can this be? Through all this, I could feel Captain watching me. Glancing back at him out of the corner of my eye, I swore he had a wickedly peculiar smirk before he quickly turned away. I have to watch him carefully; this guy could be a pervert. He could have a torture room down in his cellar.

"What happened to some of these stores? Was there a storm here?"

"A couple years ago, we had large storm hit the area. It caused widespread damage, flooding and fires. The downtown was flooded, and some places caught fire due to old electric wiring. Where have you been? It was big news around here."

Where was I, a watery purgatory, that's where! I just nodded and answered without a particle of emotion, "Oh yeah, I forgot."

Soon we arrived at Captain Joao's home. It looked like any plain vanilla ranch house. Feeling more at ease, we entered through his garage and saw an old muscle car, a blue '68 Convertible Camaro SS, being restored. What a beauty! My heart skipped a beat.

"Do you like my car. Angela is almost finished. Just a couple more tweaks here or there."

I couldn't contain my excitement. Approaching the car, I glanced over to Captain for approval to draw closer. "She's beautiful. Why do you call her Angela?"

Captain slapped my back. "Because this car was made for the angels. Go ahead. Jump in the front seat and check her out."

I sat in the driver's seat and immediately fell in love with Angela. Caressing the leather, evoked memories of Sundays with my dad, working on our own restoration projects. These mental souvenirs of happier times brought a smile to my face.

Captain took notice of my happiness. "Well, I see you love old cars. Hey, let's go in and grab a bite to eat. I'm starving."

Entering his home, I started thinking about my own Angela. What happened to her? They must have junked it to hide the evidence. The thought of her mistreatment made me angry. My blood boiled. Captain took notice of my mood and smiled.

"You hungry? How about a nice three egg Portuguese omelet with chouriço? That's my specialty. And it's pronounced sha-reese, not chorizo. You can't mispronounce the best food in the world."

"That sounds great. Can I help?"

"Sure, grab some eggs, cheese, sausage and bolos from the fridge."

Opening the fridge, I was startled to see that half of the fridge was filled with eggs. Why eggs? "Jesus, you've got a lot of eggs in here."

"Yes, I love eggs." He placed a special emphasis on *love* that was disturbing. There was also a look of exaggerated joy on face. This is weird.

Captain Joao found some old clothes in one of the unused bedrooms that he said belonged to a cousin who moved away. How lucky, they fit me perfectly. That's another red flag. The bedroom was an odd mixture of modern and antique furniture from the '40s. For a minute, I thought I was in one those old movies my mom loved.

Looking into the mirror above the bureau, I didn't see me. The reflection in the mirror wasn't my body. He looked nothing like me. Gone were my shaggy locks and slender frame. Staring back at me from the mirror was a man well over six feet tall and athletic, with a tattoo of Mother interwoven with a bleeding heart on the left side of my chest. I looked intently at my new image, wondering how this could have happened. What did it mean? Is this how a Navy SEAL looks and feels? The sight of the new tattoo steeled my nerves, as memories of my family came flooding back to me. Visualizing Mom standing next to me with a comforting gaze, I began to feel more at ease in my new skin.

My mind drifted into thoughts of revenge, no pity party for

me. Staring at my muscular new body with bewilderment, I was stronger and more imposing, completely unexpected and unrecognizable to those who would soon feel my wrath. These bastards will get the punishment they deserve, and they won't see it coming. During this revelation, Tres was with me, watching intently and barking her approval.

A murderous resolve grew inside of me as I visualized the pain and misery that I would inflict on my betrayers, and betrayal must be avenged. Blood calls for blood. Evermores will never lose again!

Captain yelled out to let me know dinner was ready. "Hey Isaac, let's eat before it gets cold. You can admire yourself again later."

How did he know what I was doing or thinking? These red flags keep on popping up. Anyway, it's time to fuel the fire.

CHAPTER 9

Spending the next two weeks assisting Captain Joao on his boat helped me get reacclimated to the real world after my watery purgatory, my best description of what it was. Work was sometimes interrupted by memories of the distress and confusion I experienced during my lost three years. I still didn't know who the voice was, but I had seen enough horror movies to make an educated guess. Trying not to think about the obvious and horrible conclusion, fishing became a welcomed diversion.

For some peculiar reason during that time, it was just Captain and me on the boat. "Hey, Captain, where are your other guys?"

Captain worked at detangling his net. "Oh, they had to go home." It struck me odd that his tone was cold and unemotional. He needed the crew before scooping me up. Questions ricocheted in my mind. Why didn't he need them now? Did he want something from me? Did he know the voice that kept me company in my watery purgatory?

With some misgivings on his response and trying to maintain a cool exterior, I needed more information. Suspicion and alertness had become my best friends, while ignorance and inattentiveness were now my enemies. No one was going to hurt me again. I would become the Alpha dog and heel for no person. "Really, where's home?"

"Down South," he said with a smirk.

My creepiness detector jumped to 10 but I shook it off for no other reason than I had nowhere else to go. Well, not yet anyway. My radar defenses remained on high alert, but I needed to get my mind straight for the task at hand.

For most of those weeks on the boat, the conversation was minimal. It was all work no play. I felt a little more at ease as each day passed. We caught plenty of fish. Who needed those other guys?

My confidence and determination at revenge grew as I peered out over the horizon each day and remembered my family. Thinking of where they were now and how they were doing awakened feelings of sadness, joy, and determination simultaneously. Memories of my mother trying to bake me a birthday cake with Yo-Yo's less than stellar culinary skills, Mom's laughter during one of our trips to the movies or working with Dad on one of his projects. All came into focus as I glanced over the horizon.

By the end of the second week, Captain Joao asked me if I wanted to talk about my traumatic boat trip. "Do you want to talk about what happened? I get the feeling that you're hiding something. You can talk to old Captain Jo-Jo. I have seen it all and I pass no judgment whatever it is. C'mon, talk to your friend. It couldn't hurt."

I had grown closer to him over the past two weeks as he never pressed me for answers. A bond of friendship had developed with Captain over that time and my radar defenses had fallen somewhat. I needed to stay alert, but I found it difficult to not trust him. He had become a good friend, or so I thought.

We even finished work on Angela; she was ready for the world. Finishing Angela's restoration reminded me of my Sundays with Dad. I was happy to hear that this time things would be different as Captain was not selling the car. When I had asked him if he was going to sell the car, his response was perfect, "What's the point if you can't enjoy the fruits of our labor."

I pondered his offer to open-up for about a minute. "What the hell. Why not, Captain."

Captain let out a huge roar of a laugh. "Good for you! Good for you!"

"Have you ever been so deceived that you still can't believe how gullible you were, even to the point when betrayal is revealed. The pain is unbearable."

With a thundering voice, Captain exclaimed, "I suffered the first deception, the one where we are taught that we can find love in the world and the world will love us back. Let me tell you, that's a lie. The universe will always create something else to love, leaving you behind, unworthy and unexceptional. If it doesn't, it will rip love from you." I could see the pain in his face and hear the trembling of his voice as he conveyed his philosophy to me. I took it, hook, line and sinker.

We shared a bond of pain and betrayal in a world rife with evil. His voice sounding even more familiar to me, I agreed with him, while he flashed a grin from ear to ear. "How did you deal with it? What can I do?"

"Well, you must meet your pain head on. Accept, nurture and be devoted to it. Let it guide you. Once you've done that, you'll never be deceived again or feel the pain of betrayal. Fulfillment and satisfaction will come once you settle your pain before it devours you."

I listened to Capitan Joao's advice and pondered my next steps. Which path do I take with my second chance in this crazy world? Ultimately, I knew what needed to be done, but first it was time to see my family. I felt strong enough to discover the impact that Jenny and the Trinity of Evil had on them after three years of torment. Halloween was approaching, the perfect time of year for mayhem and mischief.

Captain was right. I needed to meet the pain of my betrayal head on. My life and theirs would never be the same.

CHAPTER 10

The next morning, after our normal breakfast of eggs, eggs, and more eggs, Captain Joao flipped me the keys to Angela. It caught me by surprise as that car was beyond beautiful and I didn't want to ruin it. Who knew what kind of mischief I would get into that day? My plans for the Trinity of Evil, the BCs and Jenny were still in development. I didn't want to blow the opportunity for the perfect ending to my saga.

"Don't worry about the car. She'll be fine. You've earned her. Tres, go with Isaac. Make sure he doesn't get into any trouble." Captain Joao smiled as we drove to our appointment with destiny.

Captain's confidence in me made me feel 100 feet tall. I left the house for the ride across town to my old home. All along the drive there, the memories of my time with Jenny returned, as if a curtain was being pulled back across a theater screen to allow me to see the events and people more clearly. All the smug comments and deceitful machinations came roaring back in 3D. My anger grew, but this time I felt differently. My body pulsated with an infusion of an unknown energy, like a coal fed furnace on a runaway train. My head felt like it was going to split in two. Immediately, I pulled the car to the side of the road and jumped out. Panic and rage, as odd as it sounds, exploded within me. Bending over, with hands on my knees, I focused on breathing to regain my composure. Good thing I was on a side road with no witnesses. Tres kept a careful watch on me from the car. Not sure how or why, she sensed that I wasn't in any imminent danger.

The voice from my watery purgatory came back to me, "Calm down Buddy Boy. Calm Down. It's not time yet." Whoa. What was that? Relax kid. Now is not the time to freak out or to have a psychotic episode! Keep control. Think of Mom's face, her warm smile. That's it. Feeling better now. Relax kid, relax. Regaining my senses and composure, it was time to get back on the road.

Driving up that familiar street lined with old maple and oak trees, I looked for an inconspicuous place to park for my reconnaissance mission. I parked Angela across the street in a spot that had a good vantage point for spying into Dad's garage. Being Sunday, I figured he would be there fiddling around with another car. As luck would have it, he was, but to my surprise, it looked like my '69 Chevelle. Was this his way of remembering me? Did he know what happened to me? Did he look for me? My heart raced in anticipation of getting these questions answered.

More memories returned of our last Sunday together in the garage. "Dad, do you think you'll keep this one? This is a sweet pea. You should enjoy it."

"Son, there's no joy for me after it's done. Repairing and returning it to its prior glory is my joy. After we're done, someone else will be able enjoy it."

Thinking back on that day, I should have asked him why he didn't try to fix me. He released me into a cruel world, broken and full of dents. Pulling myself out of a thick fog, I noticed he was looking in my direction. Here goes nothing. I decided to interact with him to get an idea of his state of mind. I pulled the car into his driveway and came up with an excuse for being there.

My body pulsated with nervous energy as I approached my dad. "Hi, are you Mr. Evermore? I heard you like fixing old cars just like I do. So, I had to meet you. See if you can give a young guy some advice."

Dad wiped his hands, trying to remove as much grime as possible. Smiling, he extended his hand to me. "Please call me JR. Who told you about me?"

"From Benny at the auto-parts store. We were talking about my car, and he said I should talk to you, since we had common interests." I had been down to see Benny a few days ago to pick up the last remaining part for Angela. While there, I began the preliminary phase of my mission, to find an excuse to check on my family. Striking up a conversation with Benny, I had inquired about others in the area who had an interest in restoring cars and wouldn't mind comparing notes with me. Right away, he told me about my dad and how he was tinkering with his latest project. Apparently, my dad was taking it slow. That was all the information I needed at that point as I didn't want to look suspicious by inquiring too much or look like a criminal or a pervert.

"Benny's a great guy. He's helped me a lot over the years. Hey, your car is beautiful. Did you restore it yourself? How much work did you have to do?" We walked over to Angela for the first-class tour.

"My friend and I restored it. Nice team effort over many, many months. This car is a real sweet pea. Getting the original parts was a chore." Dad was startled at hearing my description of the car as a "real sweet pea". He stared at me with his mouth open to contemplate what I had just said. His reaction made me curious; so much so that I probed further. "Sorry, did I say something wrong?"

"Wow I haven't heard *sweet pea* in such a long time. It brings back fond memories." He walked around the car, admiring the finished product. "It's easy to see how much work you put into this. This is the kind of car you see on the auction shows."

We walked back over to his current project to talk about the progress he was making. As we rambled through an hour of inane banter about engines and transmissions of other cars he had restored over the years and the difficulty of getting things perfect, we forgot that it was nearly lunchtime. At several points in that amazing hour, I stared lovingly at my father and cherished the ability to reconnect with him, even though he didn't know I was his son.

Suddenly, he became teary-eyed when describing his Sundays with his son. "I used to do this with my son, Jonah, every Sunday. It was beautiful, the only way we connected like father and son. Each day, I regret not being a better father."

My body trembled at watching his emotions and hearing him express his feelings about me. "You sound as if he is no longer around. Did he pass away?"

Dad gazed downwards; a look of dejection overcame him. "We don't know. He's gone but we don't know what happened to him," his voice trembled as he caressed the car door. "His car, this car, was found abandoned at a diner about three years ago. We searched with no luck. His friends at school didn't know either. I discovered afterward that Jonah had helped Jenny, my new stepdaughter, with her studies for a bit and they had even gone out on a couple dates. That was an odd coincidence for me. I had just begun to date her mom when Jonah disappeared."

Dad, keep on thinking about Jenny, her mom and me. Connect the dots and figure it out. It's right in front of you. But he never did. He was too lost in his misery. "It sounds like you love your son very much. He's lucky to have you. I hope and pray he will come back to you from wherever he is."

To my delight and anxiety, Yo-Yo came bounding out of the house, three years older and as beautiful as she ever was. She was 17 years old by now. Could the Mannion's plan have backfired, and my family was never in danger? Maybe my dad was too strong an adversary for them? After all, he was a brilliant individual. My heart galloped with the frenzy of a new colt at the prospect that all was well with them. What joy! Could it be real?

But as Captain said, joy is momentary. Kat then stepped out of the house to call my dad in for lunch. That same energy began to pulse through my body. The voice returned, "Stay calm Buddy Boy. Stay calm."

"Hey JR, who's your friend," she asked with that same deceitful smile that I knew all too well. Her eyes gawking at my body, like a hunter for its prey. Your powers won't work on me, you pig. And I can't wait for the day you pay the butcher's bill. Motionless and on guard, Tres stared coldly at Kat.

"Hi. I'm Isaac, Isaac Noone. I work with Captain Joao on the Fisherlady for the season. He's a little shorthanded, so he asked for set of hands. We share a passion for old cars like JR does." As I was answering Kat, I could feel Yo-Yo staring at me with a puzzled look. It was the type of gaze that went right to my soul, leaving me defenseless. It was the same look she gave me during our art sessions. Did she know? How could she know? Sensing my panic, Tres bounded straight to her to create a distraction; Tres loved a good face lick. That dog seemingly knew who Yo-Yo was and wanted everyone to know she had a new friend. Yo-Yo stopped looking at me to hug her new buddy. Tres panted with satisfaction.

Kat and JR looked at the Tres and asked if she was gentle. I told them Tres was as gentle as a down pillow and she couldn't hurt a fly.

"JR, why don't you invite your new friend for lunch. We have plenty. Jenny and Riley are back from their honeymoon and they're inside waiting for us." She looked at me attentively and smiled. "Jenny is our daughter."

Dad finished wiping the last remnants of grease from his hands. "Yes, please stay. We can talk some more about cars and a future project I have in mind. I have my eyes on an old roadster I want to turn into a hot rod."

Thinking about this extended opportunity to continue our

conversation, a coldness came over me. "That sounds great. If it's not too much trouble, do you mind if I leave my dog in the back yard?"

Dad threw the greasy towel onto the hood of the car and nodded his approval. "That is no trouble whatsoever. I'll get her a water dish too."

Yo-Yo stared at me again without flinching. I held my arm out to escort her into the house. She took my arm without any reservation or apprehension. It felt like our old days together. To avoid looking excessively happy, given that I had just met everyone, I asked Yo-Yo a mundane question to refocus my mind. "Did the happy couple have a wonderful honeymoon?"

Still staring at me as we walked, Yo-Yo offered no response. We made our way into the kitchen through the side door facing the garage. I started feeling apprehensive as I made my way in. My heart raced as memories of Mom returned to me; a vision of pancakes, omelets, bacon and the aroma of cinnamon rolls came flooding back. I wasn't sure my heart could take reliving those memories.

I didn't have to worry long as I quickly noticed that my mom's kitchen was no longer her kitchen. A warm and inviting haven had been gutted and turned into a modern, cold, industrial and soulless room. It contained no warmth other than the heat from the stove. The ambient heat from our bodies or any lifeform couldn't even be retained by this stone and metal leviathan.

"Wow, beautiful kitchen, clean, functional and modern. Best I've ever seen; that's for sure." I laid on the cream nice and thick. It worked perfectly.

Kat gushed, "Thank you. This has been our labor of love. It really fits our personality and lifestyle. If you like this, you should see the rest of house. It has been completely transformed to be a modern and efficient home. Jenny, perhaps you can give Isaac a tour after lunch. Jenny, do you mind pulling your head out of the fridge for a moment to greet our guest."

My focus immediately shifted to Jenny, whose body was partially hidden by the open refrigerator door. The world seemed to slow down as she closed the door and turned toward the group.

Smiling radiantly, Jenny walked across the kitchen and stopped next to her mom. Standing with her arms crossed, her manner and response seemed somewhat abrasive for an initial introduction. "Of course, Mom. Hi, I'm Jenny. It's nice to meet you. You probably heard from my mother that we just got back from our honeymoon. So, we're looking for a nice homecooked meal after eating out for two weeks. Riley, where are you? Come in and say hello to our guest."

Jenny hadn't lost any of her physical charm and attractiveness, although I knew it belied an ugliness just underneath the surface. "It's nice to meet you as well."

Riley made his presence known with the flush of the toilet in the bathroom next to the kitchen. He came out stumbling and fixing himself. My mind went back to that day on the boat, trying to recall if Riley was the one who hit me. It didn't matter, I thought, because he was going to be first tally on the butcher's bill. His crime of marrying Jenny was enough to earn a capital punishment sentence.

Riley wiped his hands on his trousers, cementing my low opinion of him, before extending an unsanitary hand. "Hi, I'm Riley. Glad to meet you."

I returned his greeting with a respectful and unassuming handshake. "Hi, Isaac, Isaac Noone. Nice to meet you."

He strolled across the kitchen to a spot where Jenny stood. Walking behind her, he wrapped both of his arms around her, in a clear display of dominance and possession. His steely-eyed gaze was fixated entirely on me. "How do you know these guys?"

"JR and I share an interest in cars. I thought I would get some advice on a project I'm considering."

Riley answered with a smug, "Cool." Pausing momentarily, he provided me more information, "Jenny, I just got off the phone with Decker. He's busy putting the finishing touches on the pub's renovations for our grand re-opening."

Next, Kat clued me in on Decker. "Isaac, Decker is Jenny's twin brother. They recently bought the old pub in town and have been renovating it for months."

All I could muster was "Nice, can't wait to see it." My blood began to boil but it stayed below the surface. At least I know how they have been spending dad's money; home renovations and buying a pub. If it's the one I remember, the place was in rough shape.

Throughout the entire conversation and lunch, I pictured the various ways I was going to exact my bloody revenge on Decker and Riley. Shotgun? No, not painful enough. Dismembering him with a chain saw? No, too '70s horror movie-ish. Knives? Maybe. Throwing him out a window in a high-rise? Terrifying, I like it.

The lunch was mostly a kale salad mixed with quinoa and was as bland as plain fat-free yogurt. It elicited neither a feeling of human warmth nor the type of bliss that my mom's meals always did. But I played my part and ate with exuberance, complimenting the chef for a wonderful meal.

JR could only stomach the rabbit food Kat plated for him for a couple of bites before he turned his attention to me. "Isaac, tell us about yourself. How do you like working on a fishing boat?

It must be tough work."

"Not too bad. Still trying to figure out what I want to do with my life." I began to probe them for reactions, testing their awareness. "Captain calls me guppy because of my inexperience on a boat, but I seem to be a lucky charm for him." I got the reaction I wanted.

In unison, like fireworks on the Fourth of July, Jenny and the boys spat out their food and quickly brought their attention from their plates to me. Without skipping a beat, they asked, "What does he call you?" The look of shock was evident on their faces.

Kat grabbed a kitchen towel to nervously clean up their mess. "Whoa, what happened to you guys."

Happy and smiling at the result, I responded to their question. "Guppy? He's a bit of a joker. Anyway, I need to get going. I don't want to impose on you good people any longer. Perhaps, a tour of the house on another day?" I needed to get out of there before saying too much and revealing my identity or purpose too soon. Pretense was my new super-power.

"Nice meeting you all. See you soon. JR, I would love to help you with the Chevelle. The '69 is my favorite car, and it'd be cool to see her restored and back on the road."

"That sounds great," JR said with a smile. "Let's meet up in a couple days. Do you have a mobile phone?"

Damn, I forgot to get a phone. Think quick, knucklehead. "No, I am changing my service provider. My current plan is too expensive."

"OK, here's my number. Give me a call." Like I could forget my dad's mobile number. "I've been taking Wednesday afternoons off lately to focus on things around here and less on the business. Kat runs a tight ship for me."

"Thank goodness you have a great partner to take care of you." I almost threw up saying that, but I remembered her threat. She had her claws dug into him deep.

Tres and I jumped into the Camaro for the trip back to Captain Joao's house." It was a successful first day. Time to go to the mobile phone store and then to the local general store for a notepad. Got to document my plan better to avoid future mistakes. Also, did Jenny really marry her cousin? This explained a lot about the depth of the Mannion family gene pool. I could only shake my head. Tres barked her approval. It seemed strange but she knew what I was thinking.

CHAPTER 11

As we made our way back to Captain Joao's house, we took the long way through town to enjoy a scenic ride with the top down. Our drive took us by my mom's church.

Parking in front of the old building made Tres restless. The church was important to Mom; seeing it provided a flood of happy memories for me. Something about an old church brought a sense of peace and contemplation to me. It had that effect on a lot of other people too. Sitting in the car and glancing at its large front doors, I pondered my decisions and fate. Was my mission correct? Was vengeance the only answer? Was there a better way?

As I was about to drive away, I saw Sister Alicia standing with another nun and an imposing man in a side garden. They stared at me deeply and intently. For a second time in as many weeks, it occurred to me that my arrival was expected. It was very odd. Sister Alicia waved her hands in a manner that was inviting me to approach. Tres would have none of it; she barked violently and with purpose. What did Tres see that I couldn't? Why did she feel a need to protect me now?

"Girl, relax. Easy. Easy." I tried calming her down, but it wasn't working. To avoid making the evening news about a vicious dog attack on a nun, we left quickly and continued our drive back to Captain's house.

Seeing all the sights along the seashore, the old colonial architecture and town green where the local militia once drilled during the Revolutionary War brought a smile to my face. The area was quite beautiful. Everyone who saw it, had the same reaction; no matter if it were their first or one-thousandth time. The town also had a certain flavor which intensified at Halloween, most assuredly because of its involvement in the witch trials 300 years ago. While not as famous as the ones that happened in Salem, the neighboring town of Beverly's trials were still bad for the poor souls who were executed. Sometimes, being different from the pack can lead to fatal consequences. Then again, that's the universe pretending to allow you to be unique when all it wants is conformity, where the strong and beautiful rule.

Throughout the drive, I pondered my experience at the church. Why was Sister Alicia there and who were the other two people? Why were they expecting me?

The next day, Captain said we weren't going out fishing, so I had the day to myself to do anything I wanted. "Happy hunting. I'll be gone until evening. I have to run some errands to prepare for our next trip. Tres, stay with Isaac. Keep a close eye on our friend."

Having the day free, I decided to run over to the coffee shop that Jenny loved at the edge of university's campus. She had a weakness for the lattes and freshly made cranberry scones there. She would stop there before her first class in the morning. I figured on giving it a shot. Did she still have a passion for those scones? She had been away for two weeks. So, the odds were in my favor, and I had time to kill, literally.

Around 8:30, her usual time, Jenny bounded into the coffee shop looking disheveled and confused. Looks like married life wasn't agreeing with her. Quietly, I slid in behind her in line and gave her a subtle yet skillful bump.

"Oh, I'm sorry. Hey, Jenny, right?" I tried to appear as surprised as possible.

Jenny stared at me, frozen in time. I wonder if my "Guppy" comment yesterday still resonated with her. "Hey, I-Isaac, right? I didn't know you liked this coffee shop too."

Why would she? I never mentioned it. "I was told this place has the best coffee and cranberry scones in town. Or was it the only cranberry scones in town? Tres and I have the day off today. The Fisherlady isn't going out" I said with a smile. "Happy to be back home with the love of your life?"

"Huh?" Jenny was obviously startled at the question.

"You must be excited to be back home after two weeks of honeymooning. Go someplace warm I hope?"

"Y-yes. We went to Hawaii and had an amazing cruise around the Hawaiian Islands. It's a once in a lifetime type of trip."

I tried to be impressed, "Very nice. And a cruise too." As her order came to the counter, I looked to extend the conversation. I avoided drawing attention to her description of the honeymoon being a once in a lifetime type of trip. Afterall, aren't they supposed to be? "Hey, let me pay for your order? It's the least I can do after your family's hospitality yesterday." Turning to the counter, I ordered a black coffee, my usual, no milk or sugar. "Would you like to join me? I would love to hear more about the area and to get a local's perspective. My uncle – the boat's captain – wants me to relocate here to help him fulltime."

Jenny agreed to sit with me at one of the patio tables, although she failed in her attempt to look calm. We sat for a few minutes exchanging small talk about the town. Jenny's attention drifted as I spoke. She would alternatively glance at me and then distantly across the parking lot. Other times, she would gaze at Tres who had joined us from the car by then and decided to put her head on Jenny's lap begging for some serious head rubs. An uneasiness took hold of her, and I wanted to ratchet up the heat. So, I decided to test the limits of our conversation and the attractiveness of my new body. Flexing my arms ever so subtly and leaning forward, I asked, "Jenny, is everything OK? You seemed pensive yesterday, and today, you look even more preoccupied. Is something bothering you?"

"Everyday." Her response was both immediate and sorrowful.

"Me too. Sorry for the heady discussion topic early in the morning but you seem troubled."

Sensing her uneasiness softening and her defensive walls beginning to fall, I pressed further. "Have you ever thought that your life was being controlled by someone or something else, like a master puppeteer?"

Jenny could only stare at me. I struck a nerve.

"Jenny, you have the most remarkable quality about you. I can see you have a good soul. It's like we've met before, in a prior life. Not that I believe in that junk, but I feel like the guy in the poem who drowned when he tried to kiss the moon's reflection." I was about to make myself sick from all the artificial sweeteners being applied. Staying on track was critical at this point, because my prey was falling for the ruse.

Jenny giggled. I knew I had her. "Easy big fella. I have a ring on my finger. See."

"A boy can hope. Life's short and you can't blame a guy for trying."

"No, I can't," her eyes twinkled. Leaning back in her chair, Jenny became more reflective. "There is something familiar about you that I can't figure out yet. Tell me about yourself. Where are you from? Your likes and dislikes? What's your favorite movie?"

The questions kept on coming. I raised my arms, feigning surrender and laughing. "Which question do I answer first? I can count about 10. Well, you know I like fixing old cars like your stepdad. There's so much to say and so little time."

We sat and laughed for nearly an hour about various topics, as I steered her away from my personal history. For some reason, I wanted to tell her the truth. All those memories came flooding back to me, like how she could drape her golden locks over one eye to make her look more alluring, more seductive and mysterious.

I quickly regained my senses. I knew her, and her powers won't work on me anymore. Sorry, pig.

Jenny leaned forward in her chair with her eyes still sparkling. "How about we take a drive? I want to see your boat. The Fisherlady, right? Let's take your car."

"You want to see the Fisherlady? Alright, if you really

want; not sure I understand why." I had to play it cool. Jenny scooted down in the Angela's passenger seat to avoid being spotted and Tres jumped into the back.

We left on a scenic drive through town. All the Halloween decorations seemed to coalesce into my fatal enterprise. They were there to support and empower me.

When we arrived at the dock, there were only a couple of people around, just a few folks in the distant warehouses preparing to process the day's catch. All the other boats were out for the day and Captain Joao was still running his errands. Now it was time to be the requisite gentlemen. I extended my hand and gently helped her onto the boat, which was spectacularly ordinary looking. The Fisherlady was nothing special, a nondescript fishing trawler that was fit for purpose, like a glove for a hand.

Unsteady on her feet, Jenny stumbled as she lifted her leg over the side. Whether the fall was staged or real, I was there to catch her. "Whoa. Are you ok? I got you. Easy now."

I held onto her longer than necessary, but she didn't seem to mind. What was her game? Was she that much of a whore, who would cheat on her husband two weeks after getting married, or was she probing to find out more about me, since I made her nervous? I figured it was more of her whorish side coming out, and I was right. Jenny angled her head to kiss me. Her reaction was nothing like I experienced with her before. She seemed to enjoy this more. Skipping over the trivialities and minor details, we moved to an inside cabin and took our passion to the next level on Captain's bunk. Boy, was she ready! I figured, why not get some hoo-ha action before she's worm food. My power increased with each evil thought put into action. Let's just say I liked my new physique and power, and so did Jenny.

We reclined there for a while thinking of what we just did. Jenny plied me with crocodile tears, telling me she didn't like how her life turned out. She's good, really good. "You must think I'm a total slut, but I'm not. Something hit me when I met you yesterday and you have been on my mind since then. I just wanted to feel good for the first time in three years."

"No, I understand. You're obviously unhappy. Did something happen to you?"

Sometimes, family can be a burden. I wish," pausing momentarily, Jenny continued her thought, "that I was free, free of being bound to family history." Her eyes teared up and her voiced trembled. "They don't care for anyone except for themselves. I'm just a pawn, a ragdoll, or like the puppet you described, to be used and enjoyed, then put away. Other times, I feel like a zombie sleepwalking through life."

Boy, she was still good at the game. She's using one of my old lines! I listened with intent and focus, not impressed by her whining, all the while trying to find potentially new avenues for completing my mission of punishing my betrayers. But what did Jenny want? Where was she going with this?

Rising from the bunk to put on my pants and to hand Jenny her clothes, I considered her perspective. "Family can be a burden. Too bad we can't eliminate them from our lives. Hey, it's getting late. Let me take you back before anyone misses you."

"No one will miss me. Family is worse than a burden; they are a life sentence. You know, I married my cousin. My cousin! My family brings the meaning of the Theory of Relativity to a whole new level. Thanks for being so cool today. Maybe we can meet again tomorrow or something." Jenny glanced at me sheepishly, hoping to get a positive response.

"Sure, that would be great. This was the nicest day I've had in three years too. Give me your number and I'll give you a call." Even though I knew her number, I had to ask. Got to keep up appearances.

Jenny gave her number to me, and then asked me an odd question. "Did anyone ever mention that you smell like cinnamon rolls?" Jenny asked the question in a manner that was more yearning than inquisitive, which left her appearing somewhat vulnerable to me.

"No, but it's good to know," I replied with a laugh.

"Don't laugh at me. There's something about you so familiar and warm that I find both comforting and terrifying. You must think I'm crazy."

"Everyone fears the unknown. You're human, just like me." A feeling of satisfaction came over me as I drew her deeper into my snare.

I dropped Jenny off at the coffee shop, avoiding a kiss so as not to attract attention. I think I may prolong her torment a few more days. She thinks she has me under control. She has a rude awakening coming. Next, I needed to get a new phone.

CHAPTER 12

After buying a new mobile phone, a burner that wouldn't be easily traceable, I went to bed that evening with the satisfaction that my plan was working. The groundwork had been laid and my victims, I mean the guilty, would begin to feel my wrath. Before I fell into a deep sleep, the notion that Jenny was a pawn in this drama entered my mind. Was her story another element of this tragedy, another tributary feeding our wretched drama? Or was she just playing me? I'd have to wait a little while longer to complete my revenge epic and know the answer to this question.

Anyway, arising around noon the next day, I stumbled into the kitchen, where Captain Joao was sitting enjoying one of his malodorous cigars. Half yawning and scratching my new and improved manhood, I asked, "Why didn't you wake me?

"He's alive. Lazarus has risen." His bellowing tone was not lost on me as he raised his arms to the heavens. A deaf person could hear it. "Good afternoon, how was your day? Looking at how long you slept, it must have been really, really good." He said with a wink.

How did he know? He suddenly got creepy again. Half awake, I asked, "No fishing today?"

"No fishing. The part I need for the boat will take a couple more days to fabricate. The boat needs a special part before we can go back out to sea. You're free to do whatever you want to do for a couple more days. Did you get a new phone at the place I told you about?"

"Yup, all set. What's for breakfast, or is it brunch time now? You didn't get home before I went to bed and I'm sick of eggs. I haven't eaten since yesterday morning."

Captain clasped his hands in mock prayer. "Pobre menino. You can't figure out dinner on your own?"

Aggravated and not yet fully awake, I rested my head in my hands at the kitchen table. "No Portuguese please."

"Hey, let's go out for lunch. I've been craving double dough pepperoni pizza from Giuseppe's Kitchen all week. What do you think?"

Alright now, there's coincidence and then there's living in my head. My radar is on high alert but damn I'm hungry. He hit me at a weak spot in my defense shield, pepperoni pizza. "That sounds great. Let's go."

Leaving Tres at home, we drove over to the restaurant, lickety split. The anticipation and hope I felt for recapturing those fond memories of Saturdays with Mom grew with each turn. Would the aroma of pizza and calzones be too much for me to handle? Those long idle memories began to stir more within me.

As we entered Giuseppe's Kitchen, I recalled an old memory of my mom sitting at one of the far tables. I knew it was just a specter of the past, a memory of one of our Saturdays resurrecting itself at the perfect time. Waving to me, she sat holding a slice of pizza with a giant smile on her face. Seeking solace for my still grieving heart, I walked toward her. A son can never truly get over the loss of his mother. To me, we would always have that invisible umbilical cord connecting life, hope and maternal love. A queen on earth and now a queen in heaven, Mom always thought of her children first and foremost.

Ruining the moment, Captain Joao slapped me on the back, pulling me from my daydream. "What's wrong? Seeing ghosts?"

"You know you're beginning to annoy me."

We ordered a whole tray from Giuseppe's daughter, Emily. She used to waitress on the weekends to help her dad. It appeared nothing had changed. Emily was always nice to my mom and me. She was a good kid and Yo-Yo's classmate.

We ate an entire tray of pizza, which is amazing considering it's the thick Sicilian type that comes in pans of 16 slices. Nothing better than that, period. The rectangular trays Giuseppe used must be at least 50 years old, absorbing five decades of olive oil and flavor with each new creation. The waitress couldn't believe we finished the whole order and washed it down with a 6-pack.

Cleaning the table, Emily raised her eyebrows and expressed her admiration. "Well done boys. I'll never doubt you guys again." Pausing slightly, then regaining her senses, she asked, "Hey, does anyone smell cinnamon rolls? This is so odd. We don't have any on the menu and I distinctly smell cinnamon rolls." She looked right at me with the same look in her eyes that Jenny had yesterday, as if she were in some sort of trance.

That's the second time in as many days. Did I become some sort of a human fragrance diffuser? Both times when the aroma surfaced, I was in a happy mood. Was happiness causing me to release a fragrance of cinnamon rolls to attract my prey? Is this another special power? Regardless, I needed to be aware of it.

Captain responded, "Yes, we just made some this morning for the crew. We probably overdid it with the cinnamon." He knew, but how? The mystery of my story continued to grow.

We departed quickly to avoid bringing attention to ourselves. Emily remained standing alone, trying to recover her senses.

I was puzzled at what just happened. "Captain, what was that?"

"Isaac, some guys got it, and some guys don't. You got it." Captain laughed the whole ride home.

I understood certain changes to me could be used to satisfy my growing lust for vengeance. There was a score to settle, and the universe required that life's balance sheet be leveled. Blood calls for blood. My new body was a weapon with a skill to lure people into a state of vulnerability and make them defenseless to my charms. They will succumb to my planned manipulations. But what other powers did I have? Why this body? Was it a shell or illusion? Could I change it? These questions reverberated through my mind; all the while Captain laughed throughout the entire ride home. He was really annoying me now. I need to invest in noise cancelling headphones.

CHAPTER 13

After Captain regained his composure, it was quiet enough to call Jenny to see if we could set up another round of passion, along with the aroma of a heavy dose of cinnamon rolls. Jenny didn't pick up because I assume she did not recognize the number. I left a voice mail.

"Hey, this is Isaac. What's going on? Looking for that special house tour." I regretted leaving such a lame message as soon as I hung up.

It only took a few minutes for Jenny to call back. "Hey, I'm happy you called. I've been thinking about yesterday all day. It was something that brought me back to a time when I was truly happy. Sorry for getting corny, but it felt like I was awakened from a bad dream. Only to realize, the nightmare was real when I got back home. You there? Did I lose you?"

"I'm here. Just taking it all in. You sound like you've

been through one hell of an ordeal. If you want to talk about it, I'm here to listen, judgement free."

"You must think I'm a complete psycho, unloading all this crap on you after only one day."

"Not at all, life is a balancing act, a sort of scale. If we put too much weight on one side, the scale crashes. I've learned that removing some weight will restore equilibrium for me." If she only knew what I meant by removing some weight.

"Can we meet tonight? At the boat? Decker and Riley will be busy at the pub, getting it ready for opening night."

I could barely contain my joy. "Sure. 7:00? I'll bring dinner."

Jenny's response sent an electric shock through my body. "Yummy. That sounds wonderful. See you there. What do you want to eat?"

"Don't worry. I'll figure out something."

With the afternoon free, I decided to take a drive to think about Jenny's call. Was she a pawn, victim or a liar? She couldn't be that good an actress. Doubts echoed in my mind until I found myself in front of my mom's old church again. Since Tres wasn't with me, I decided to go in, figuring it couldn't hurt. Clutching my medal of St. Michael, I pushed open the ancient oak doors that must have weighed a ton. You figure they would make it easier to get in, rather than appearing to keep people out.

I could hear faint voices, unlike the others who baby sat me for three years. These were new and less creepy. "He's here. He's here. The beast has not won. The wolf still fights. Yes, he can still come back to us."

A sense of turmoil stirred in me as I walked up the aisle toward the alter, stopping halfway to slide into a pew, another word that would make Yo-Yo laugh. She would say, "What's wrong with it? Does it smell or something?" I began to laugh softly; Yo-Yo always brought a smile to my face.

A familiar voice came from behind me. "Well, young man, it's nice to see you in here."

Startled, I was surprised to see Sister Alicia. "Oh, hi. You scared me."

Sister Alicia carried a large candle in her arms that she was bringing over to a side alcove. "I doubt that a large and imposing man such as you can scare easily. What brings you in today my child?"

"Just looking for some peace and quiet. Please, can I help you with that? I don't want to see you fall." Taking the candle from Sister Alicia, we walked together to the alcove. I placed it into an empty holder next to an imposing statue of St. Jude, the patron saint of lost causes and an appropriate stop for me that day. I searched for a way to terminate the conversation, but she wouldn't let it end.

Sister Alicia accompanied me as I continued my trek to the altar. "We all have a desire for peace and quiet; the way we go about achieving it can be as different as day and night. Are you in the daylight or night, Mr. Evermore?"

Panic gripped me. How did she know my name? "Evermore? You have me confused with someone else. My name is Isaac."

Interrupting me, Sister Alicia interjected, "Yes, I know. Isaac Michael Noone. We have to admit, that's a good one, I. M. No One."

My panic rose a level. "We?"

Coming from behind us, seemingly out of nowhere, was the other nun and large fellow I saw the other day. The latter had the appearance of a bodyguard. The nun responded quickly, "Us."

She had a soft face with gentle eyes that offered comfort. Her gaze had a maternal quality about it. The other guy was imposing, taller than me, and stared at me with a coldness that ran shivers up and down my spine.

"And who are you?" My anxiety building, I wanted to get out of there quickly.

The nun raised her hands, palms up, to show she was not a threat. "Don't worry Jo-Jo. It's Jo-Jo right? That's what your mom called you."

Rising to my feet, feeling incensed and provoked, I responded, "What! Don't you dare bring up my mom."

Her guardian, the best description I have of him, approached me with an intention of ripping my head off, or so it seemed. The nun held her hand to his chest and told him, "It's alright. Jo-Jo wouldn't try to hurt me. Would you Jo-Jo?"

"OK, easy Tiny." I started calling him Tiny, hoping to get a laugh out of him. He didn't like it, but I sat back down to diffuse the situation as my anger subsided upon hearing her speak. How could anyone hurt or want to hurt her? I gazed at the floor in shame. She wasn't the enemy. The evil people, who had caused me so much pain, were the focus of my wrath. These three were not the ones who killed Mom and were tormenting Dad and Yo-Yo. If she were here, my mom wouldn't be happy with me right now.

"I am the Mother Superior. Most people just call me Mother. I work with the less fortunate to find their way in the world. Often, we work with God's grace to help people see the beauty in life and creation, especially the misguided and those who believe they are not worthy of love."

I tapped into the indignation growing within me, "Creation? Did God create evil people, or does He allow them to exist? I've heard it all before. God is Love. Whatever! The world needs a kick in the pants. But wait a minute, how do you know my real name?" It took a few seconds to register that she had called me Jo-Jo. How did she know? What did they know?

Mother Superior placed her hand on Tiny's arm to ensure he maintained his calm. "I know your mom. Pure spirits like your mom bring light into the world."

This revelation was a jolt to my sanity. I could only stare at her in shock. "You mean you knew my mom."

"I meant what I said. Jo-Jo, you are at a tipping point. You can't be judge, jury and executioner for the sins that plague the world. You believe you can battle against those fatal sins, which are loved by the beast and tear humanity from grace. That's your mission, isn't it, to fatally punish the wicked? You're wading deeper and deeper into the darkest depths of the abyss, eventually losing that light everyone was given at birth. There are better ways. Captain Joao knows this, but he is unwilling to see the truth." The pontificating continued to my irritation.

"Life has three unbreakable parts, a three-dimensional

bond. Some know it as the Father, Son and Holy Ghost, others call it the trinity of heaven, earth, and the spirit, the ethereal connection that anchors all things together into the divine. We need to foster that connection with the virtues bestowed by heaven, that delicate balance between a celestial presence and physical world. No matter how you view it, we are the caretakers of that bond. Abusing it and accepting the beast's way, can cause a ripple effect of suffering that only cultivates and nurtures evil. Wrath is not justice. We can't...."

I couldn't take the theological lecturing anymore. Frustrated, I rose to leave, gently though, as I didn't want to upset her gargantuan friend. "With all due respect, I tried your way, and look where it got me."

Sister Alicia yelled to me as I walked away quickly, "Don't give up. Learn to love yourself. Please Jo-Jo."

Outside the church and across the street, I saw a large wolf sitting and looking in my direction. Motionless, it was taking a measure of me before it ran off. What was a wolf doing around here? Should I follow it? Those faint whispers returned. "We failed. He should have been better prepared for the battle."

The three of them stood on the church steps with looks of great concern as I drove away. Well two did; Tiny still had the cold look of a man who wanted to beat me senseless. I could see they were talking to each other as I peeked into the rearview mirror, with Mother Superior giving Sister Alicia a comforting hug. I could see she was in distress, but why? Her shoulders caved in; Sister Alicia looked like someone whose entire life was destroyed. Why was Sister Alicia so affected by our conversation? She never showed this emotion to me, or for me, before.

I drove back to Captain Joao's house, replaying the interaction countless times, wondering what it all meant. Who were they? What were they talking about? I detected something different about them, an indescribable quality that felt more supernatural than natural, if that makes sense. Perhaps, my new body came with an enhanced sort of radar. I wished it came with a manual.

The faint whispering voices returned, "Jo-Jo, where are you going? Beware of the beast. Beware."

What part did these voices have in relation to my mission? The beast? The wolf? Did my transformation include becoming a spiritual zookeeper? I needed a nap!

After a quick siesta, I stopped by Giuseppe's Kitchen to pick up dinner; a side salad drizzled in balsamic, a chicken parmigiana sub with the fixings piled so high it bordered on ludicrous, and two Diet Dr. Peppers. This was Jenny's favorite meal; one we had always split prior to and after pursuing our intellectual and physical pursuits for the night.

In the restaurant parking lot, a man was berating his wife and young kids for a silly transgression, their existence. Everyone could hear him telling his family how he had nothing and how all his dreams had been destroyed. Their existence played a factor in his failures. Losing his job was the latest example of his crumbling life. Leaving his wallet home, he couldn't order dinner for his family. This was an embarrassment that sent him over the edge.

"Don't you see, I'm no good. And with you, I'm worse and you're worse. You're better off without me." His wife cried, begging him to stop.

The children quaked with fear at the sight of their out-of-control father. "Please daddy, no. We'll be good. Please daddy, no." They hugged their mother closely and looked for her maternal protection.

I walked over full of rage and with punishing intent. As he was about to strike his wife, I grabbed hold of his arm, but instead of striking him, the world suddenly froze in place. People in the parking lot seemed like statues, motionless except for me and the person about to feel my wrath.

He wailed, "What is this? Who are you?"

I must admit I was confused for a moment, but like a dam being breached by a raging flood, I released a torrent of flashing images and a cacophony of screams, making him experience the pain his wife and children felt. "Who am I? I am Mayhem. Wrath. Vengeance. I am Chaos. I am here to judge you." Looking at my victim, I pondered whether he truly deserved my planned punishment, one that would bring grave results. There was a sense of a man in turmoil who needed to be shown a better path. Punishing him would also penalize his family. I recalled Mother's comment on the ripple effect of suffering. It had weighed on me. Sometime later, I would come to realize this as the ongoing battle between the beast and wolf for my soul.

As these images rushed through his mind, he also felt the punishment I was about to give him. "What do you choose; the hand that helps or punishes?" I motioned an extended hand of friendship and the other one clasped tightly to his arm to make my point clear. "Look at your family. You are their protector, their knight. They need you. Cherish them and they will be the most precious gift a man could ever want. Whenever a child says that most beautiful word, dad, to a father, he understands true joy. Family is our backbone and children are our hearts. Both need to be cherished, or else you will have to deal with me."

He genuinely expressed sorrow, crying, "I'm so sorry. I was so angry, angry at the world and my life. I lost sight of what was important. I've been a loser in everything I've tried to do or achieve. They deserve a better father than me. My family is irreplaceable. I deserve to be punished."

Contemplating my response as the man continued his mutterings of a life wasted, I looked deeply at the heart and soul of this person. Here was a man who was beaten down by life and more so by himself. Driven to rage because he couldn't fit into a perceived model of success, he gave up on life. Was I seeing a reflection of my future-self if I hadn't died at a young age? Rage was the easy answer for responding to his failings that day. Erupting like a long dormant volcano, emotionally suppressed and boiling for years, he had unleashed a torrent of anger.

"A loser in everything you do! Look at your family. Do you really think they feel that way? They are frightened of life with you and without you. Cherish them and you'll be the richest man in the world. If you can't love yourself, love them. See yourself as they see you."

At that point, I released him and moved away, electing not to punish him further as his contrition was genuine. He turned to his family, still looking stunned, and embraced them with the strength of a grizzly bear. "I'm so sorry. I know I need to be better. Please help me. You are the most precious things in my life."

It brought me great satisfaction seeing the family hug and cry in a renewed feeling of joy and commitment. The rest of the parking lot seemed dazed, looking at each other in confusion and not knowing what had happened.

While satisfied at the outcome of my intervention, I stood in the parking lot and reflected on the events that brought me to this point in my life. My life? It's an odd thing to say, considering my current state, but it's the best description I had. New powers were revealing themselves; however, a more positive philosophy about life and the world at large had emerged. The experiences during my isolation in the watery purgatory and the events of the past several weeks had brought on this transformed vitality and perspective. My mom's teachings and compassion had taken effect, if only it hadn't taken an extreme act of betrayal to recognize them. In my heart, I had always known she was right, but a teenager lost in his own melancholy and unbending sensibilities had made me less receptive to admitting it. Maybe time travel could reveal itself as my next superpower? Wishful thinking, I guess. Regardless, a new philosophy had emerged, and Mom was its foundation. A decision between accepting vengeance or providing compassion continued to rage inside me. What path would I choose? Or was there a fate where both resided?

I could hear the whispers again, "The beast doesn't have him yet. We still have a chance." The battle between my two internal foes, my spiritual battle buddies, would escalate in the coming weeks. Buckle up folks, the ride's about to get rough.

Jenny was waiting for me at the Fisherlady, and she looked as beautiful as ever. I hid behind a wall leading to one of the fish wholesalers and spied on her for a few minutes to see if I could catch her doing something guilty. I watched her closely, but nothing happened. Jenny sat on a bench by the pier with a contemplative look, shoulders down with the weight of the world on her. At that moment, confusion governed me. My two battling buddies went AWOL and wouldn't be helping me tonight. I was on my own.

I walked slowly to where Jenny was sitting. The yard was exceptionally quiet, as all the boat crews were done for the night and only the monotonous sounds of the harbor buoys' bells could be heard. Lost in her thoughts, Jenny was clearly preoccupied, and she didn't see me approaching, unless my prior invisibility superpower had mysteriously been reenergized. Jenny jumped with a shriek when I touched her shoulder.

Her arms flailing, Jenny cried out, "Ahhh! Holy crap."

"Sorry," I said with a laugh.

"Give me a minute to compose myself. I may need to change my underwear. Yikes." She began laughing a soft subtle giggle that showed her silly side, and one that only came out when we were alone. I remembered our relationship more fondly. My focus faded from revenge to compassion. She genuinely appeared to be in turmoil and in a state of mind that rivaled my pre-Jenny world. My mission hit a detour and a mobile phone app wasn't available to get me back on track.

"Jenny, where were you just now? You seemed to be a million miles away, lost in your thoughts."

"I was just thinking," her voice tailed off as she faded into another funk "that I wish my life had come out differently. I have caused a lot of pain, irreversibly and irreparably in one particularly terrible situation."

Sensing an opportunity, I probed her for more information. "Do you want to talk about it? People say I'm a good listener."

Gathering herself, Jenny thought it better to not talk about it further. "No, that's OK. I talk too much. Mom keeps on reminding me that I have a problem with my inner monologue control switch." Regardless, a further exploration of her trauma and emotions was justified in my eyes.

"Well, here's dinner, a side salad drizzled in balsamic, a chicken parmigiana sub with the fixings piled high, and two Diet Dr. Peppers."

I got the reaction I was looking for. Jenny's eyes popped wide open at the sight of dinner as it obviously brought back memories of our study dates. "How did you know that's my favorite dinner? And from Giuseppe's, no less?"

"Wow, that's my favorite too. Cap turned me on to these, and I can't stop eating them." That should keep her mind at ease for now. Don't want to accidentally give my disguise away to early.

We went back into the cabin and had an evening of food and nooky. I felt alive again. It was difficult to conceal my joy; however, it battled with a feeling of sadness when images of Yo-Yo would enter my mind. Did I become a traitor, a collaborator with the Mannions? Making love to Jenny filled me with indescribable joy, and her passion for me seemed authentic. We became one body physically and spiritually, a rapturous feeling we shared during my prior incarnation as Jo-Jo.

After this marathon session of love, we reclined in Captain's bunk. Jenny rested her head on my chest and shifted the conversation. "I love your tattoo. What does it mean?" She asked, while slowly caressing the tattoo's outline.

"It keeps my mom alive. She died of cancer a few years ago. She was the light of my life." Talking about her brought tears to my eyes.

"That is so sweet to have had someone in your life as special as your mom was. But it's so sad you lost her. Life sucks. That medal around your neck. It seems familiar to me. I had a dear friend who had one just like it."

I made sure to sound and look surprised at the revelation. "Oh yeah? What happened to him? It sounds like he's past tense."

"It was JR's son, Jo-Jo. We dated for a bit in college, a nice kid with a big heart." Jenny continued to caress my heart tattoo while she continued her story. "Jo-Jo was a quiet boy who thought less of himself than others did. I fell for him, not at first, but there was something about him that appealed to me. Like a moth to a flame, I was attracted to his innocence and purity. We still don't know what happened to him." Her voice began to tremble.

Seeing her fade away again, I wanted to change the subject, "Wow, quite a guy for sure. Tell me about JR and Yo-Yo. They seem like nice people."

"How did you know we call her Yo-Yo?"

I slipped up again. Thinking quickly, I responded to prevent any further suspicion, "JR called her that. Am I mistaken?"

"No, you're right."

Whew, that was close.

"My mom and JR fell in love after the death of their spouses. I guess they needed each other to get through the grief. My dad was the nicest guy you could ever meet, never a bad word about anyone and always positive. He told me he loved me every day. When he died, the world crashed onto me, and I still haven't dealt with it properly."

"He sounds like he was a great guy." Too bad he married a person who will soon be sent to hell.

"Yeah, JR is a really nice guy, quiet and very talented at inventing things, although my mom has him wrapped around her finger. She rules the roost. There are days I feel sorry for him. She treats him like a Marine drill instructor does a raw recruit. I think she's the original Karen. She treats Yo-Yo the same way. Keeps her close at home and doesn't want to give her any independence. It's like a prison for her."

My rage grew. Keeping Yo-Yo in such a manner would break her spirit eventually. Let's hope it isn't too late. Changing the subject, I inquired about the pub. "When is the pub opening? I would love to drop by."

Shocked at the possibility of going to the opening, Jenny leaped from the bunk to emphasize her surprise. "Really, no! You wouldn't like to socialize with those two jackasses."

"Don't worry. It'll be fine." It was revealing how Jenny thought of her brother and cousin-husband.

Jenny scratched her head, dumfounded at my desire to attend. "Well, I warned you. They have a soft opening Thursday night. The whole family will be there."

I got up and joined Jenny in an embrace to relieve her concerns. "I promise to behave, no worries from me. It sounds like it will be a fun night. Anyway, you should get home before you're missed."

Trying to extend the evening for as long as possible, I dressed slowly. Disconnecting from Jenny was still not easy to do. Jenny noticed my slow pace and offered her assistance. After she had finished getting dressed, Jenny moved slowly back to help me. "OK big fella, we need to go."

She was both seductive and sweet as she maneuvered a belt around my waist, showing her affectionate and alluring sides simultaneously. Time stopped for a moment as we gazed intently into each other's eyes. She placed her head on my chest again to gently caress my tattoo. "Isaac, please promise you won't ever hurt me. I've had too much of that in my life."

Her sincerity hit me hard. She couldn't be acting. There's no way that she could have been lying to me. "Never. I will never hurt you."

My quest for vengeance became a lower priority. I fell back in love with Jenny, or perhaps my love for her was transformed like this physical form I now inhabited. For the first time since my rebirth several weeks earlier, I felt vulnerable, and it was enjoyable. Was I being tricked again? Just when I thought I had this all figured out, Jenny threw me a curve ball. I needed more answers, and I knew where to get them.

CHAPTER 14

Captain Joao was waiting for me, albeit not very patiently, to return home. As soon as I walked in, the inquisition started. "Isaac, I'm in the kitchen. Please come here. We need to talk."

I walked into the kitchen and sat at the table opposite where Captain was sitting, not suspecting what was going to come next. "What's up?"

With a stern voice, he bellowed, "So, it appears you had a busy day today. Did you meet with anyone special?" The muscles in his face began to flex in and out as he clamped down tight on his jaw.

"I had a very good day. What's it to you?" My contempt for his question was immediately recognizable in my response and my facial expression. While he had been good to me up to this point, I didn't like being questioned.

"Listen," his tone softening, "I don't want to see you led astray by fake promises and religious mumbo jumbo. I know you went by the church today. It's time we have a good talk about our place in this world, and for you to understand who we are." He emphasized *we* heavily.

"What do you mean, who we are? I know who I am. Who do you think you are?" My annoyance grew. He couldn't see my fists clenched tightly under the table.

Captain banged his fist on the kitchen table to emphasize his irritation with me. "Jo-Jo, enough. Please listen to my story."

He knew my real name! My jaw dropped at the revelation. I nodded my head, signaling my agreement to his request, and the Ballad of Captain Joao Carvalho began, an interesting contribution and detour for my journey.

Captain began his story, theatrically raising his arms to emphasize the grandeur of his tale. "I was born in Lisbon in the year 1480, or it could have been a year earlier. The record keeping wasn't great back then. That's right, about 540 years ago. The exact year of my birth isn't really known, but it's around that time. I was known throughout the Iberian Peninsula as a master sailor, Captain and navigator. People would say I had salt water, and not blood, in my veins. The sea was a welcoming home for men wanting adventure and mischief. There's nothing more spectacular than a sunset seen from a ship's bow on the open seas. The colors from the setting sun would fill the sky. It would make a person believe in God and look at life on land as a punishment.

My ships sailed throughout European waters, the Mediterranean, the Atlantic and beyond. We sailed to many foreign and exotic lands, fearlessly in search of profit, and business was good, although a little bloody. Portugal ignited an Age of Discovery with a fever not seen for a thousand years. We were the center of the universe. We were gods.

I had a lust for life, drinking and whoring wherever our ships sailed, and never concerned about the consequences. On duty, I was all business. Off duty, I was an animal, a carnivore who would screw anything that wasn't nailed down in each port. Pleasure was sought and obtained, bought and paid with the trade profits from the goods acquired in the lands we visited. Visited isn't the right word for describing our time in each port. It was an invasion of mind, body and soul. I was the poster boy for the Seven Deadly Sins, well maybe four or five anyway. There's one or two that can be debated. It's amazing my friend, Pedro, didn't fall off." Pointing to his crotch, Captain snickered at that last comment.

I was physically revolted at the thought. "Seriously, Captain. That's disgusting. And you gave it a name? I can't get it out of my head now. Thanks a lot."

Captain raised hands in a manner that admitted he crossed a line. "Sorry. Sorry. Let's return to my story. At the end of the 15th century, I was a young crew member on one of the ships that sailed with Vasco de Gama to India, under the orders of the king to find a sea route to the East and to the ancient kingdoms of India. We were serving God and country. The Muslims, along with the Venetians, controlled the overland trade routes and the trading ports in the Indian Ocean. The king wanted our navy to establish Portuguese control of the trade and cut out the Muslim merchants and Venetians from the equation. Everyone was getting rich; we wanted our piece too. The prize was spice, which was worth its weight in gold. Spices such as turmeric, cinnamon, salt and believe it or not, pepper were some of the prizes we sought for trade back home. The jewels weren't bad either.

We sailed south from Lisbon, past the Canary and the Cape Verde Islands, around the Cape of Good Hope before landing in Mozambique on the Eastern shores of Africa. We left stone markers in many of the places we landed to tell the world that Portugal had been there, like astronauts planting the flag on the moon. Many are still there today.

Within a few months, we arrived in the Kingdom of Calicut, the domain of the Zamorins in western India on the coast of Malabar. Zamorins were powerful rulers and fearsome warriors were not to be taken lightly. Powerful Muslim merchants controlled and protected the ports of Malabar under the authority of the Zamorins. Our goal of achieving dominance of the spice trade was not going to be an easy one.

Entering the port of Calicut, the local population looked at us suspiciously, not knowing who we were or why we had come. Even though our intentions were not pure, we tried to convince the population of our innocence. After some time, we were allowed an audience with the Zamorin monarch. We weren't prepared for the opulence and grandeur of the court; gold and jewels surrounded the exquisitely decorated Zamorin throne. The sights and customs of the Zamorin ruler and his people were astounding and humbling to poor country boys from Portugal. Our first trip to this exotic land wasn't financially profitable, but it taught us that we needed to up our game. We failed to consider how advanced Calicut would have been. They weren't fans of the trinkets we brought for trade, although they did trade some spices with us to take home. I think they took pity on us for being less refined. The major benefit of our first voyage was the fever of adventure and profit it ignited in us and in me. I promised to return someday, but the next time it had be as a captain of my own ship. My pride would not accept any other option.

For the next 10 years, my focus was improving my maritime skills and earning a Captaincy, so that my return trip to Calicut would be a memorable one. This time, however, I would be captaining a fearsome Man O' War, not a mere merchant vessel but the fiercest fighting ship in the world. There was an obstacle in our way preventing us from becoming masters of the spice trade. We knew that we had to deal with the deeply entrenched and rich

Muslim merchants and their navy.

My return coincided with a famous sea battle that would make us masters of the Arabian Sea, the Battle of Diu. Our noses were bloodied the year before at the Battle of Chaul. At Diu, Portugal sailed a great armada to fight against a combined Muslim and Calicut fleet who had the financial backing of the Venetian Republic. The Zamorin of Calicut, who had always treated us with some suspicion, wanted us gone. In the years between our first visit and the battle, there were various incidents and skirmishes that damaged our relationship with the Zamorin. Additionally, the Venetians saw us a threat to their lucrative trade deals with the Muslim merchants. So, the stars were aligned against us.

Under the command of Admiral Dom Francisco de Almeida, we battled against this three-party coalition. Our confidence was high. We had modern warships with the most lethal technology of the day. Approaching their battle formation, we noticed a flaw in their strategy. They had held some of their galleys in a passage leading out of the harbor in an apparent battle tactic to hit us from behind. Yes, galleys were still used, as they were in the Battle of Lepanto some years earlier. Noticing their plan, I quickly maneuvered my ship into a placement now referred to as *Crossing the T,* blocking the passageway for the galleys, and ordered our guns to open fire. What's the expression? It was like shooting fish in a barrel. Their cannons and ships were no match for our weaponry.

It was a total victory, making us the masters of the Arabian Sea as well as the Indian Ocean. A year later, Afonso de Albuquerque captured Goa which afforded us a naturally defensible port to create our empire in India. Several years and battles later, we signed a treaty with the Zamorin to establish a fort in Calicut. It is here that I met my Aanshi, a princess of the court who possessed a tender soul and had unrivaled beauty. Upon my first sight of her, I was thunderstruck.

While de Albuquerque promoted a plan for the Portuguese to marry the local women of Goa as a way of solidifying our position on the continent and converting locals to Christianity, my attachment to the princess would be unique and challenging to say the least. During the ceremony to sign the treaty, I caught my first glimpse of Aanshi. Leading an endless line of attendants and courtiers into the hall where the ceremony was to take place, she appeared to be gliding on air more so than walking. The crowd bowed their heads to solemnly recognize her presence. As she passed me, my head remained bowed. Stopping for a moment, she asked, 'So, are you the great sea captain I have heard so much about? You must regale us with tales of your adventures.'

Standing in front of her, dressed in the best clothes imaginable for court but feeling like a fish out of water, I remained motionless and speechless, unable to form words. Aanshi laughed so sweetly and delightfully at my reaction that I still have her glowing face pictured in my mind to this day. I tripped through a response, something like, "Y-Y-Yes, princess. It would be my ah…ah….honor." So smooth!

Aanshi smiled as she walked away. During the signing ceremony, I fidgeted with my collar, still acting like a little schoolboy, but it was hot that day. Every so often, Aanshi would glance over at me, further enchanting me with each smile. After the ceremony, I noticed that she was whispering to one of her attendants while secretly pointing toward me. My heart began to race at the thought of speaking to her. My anticipation and excitement level reached a height greater than any I had previously experienced, even those before any of my sea battles, not that I'm comparing the similarity of the emotions between love and war. Sometimes, however, these emotions can feel the same in certain situations. So, I guess I am. Let's not go down that rabbit hole.

We met later in the palace garden, chaperoned by her attendants. There was no funny business, if you know what I mean. She told me stories of her life and family. For hours, I wouldn't say a word, because listening to the sweet melody of her voice was all that I needed. Imagine a person like me falling for a princess! The difficult part came when Aanshi asked me about my life, home, and family. I knew lying to her was not an option. I had grown to love her, that's right love her.

Baring my soul, I spoke of my humble beginnings in Portugal, the son of loving parents and brother to three crazy sisters. We didn't have a lot of money, but we were happy. Aanshi heard about my boyhood dream to become a captain and to see, no, to devour the world. I embraced my desires with the immaturity of youth and never looked back. After a few minutes of storytelling, or should I say an act of contrition, I could see Aanshi's physical and mental recoil to my stories, but something odd happened. Aanshi did not run from me. She wanted to know how I felt now about my life. 'Do you think these experiences have made you the person you want to be.'

What a question? My response was simple, as her comforting gaze made me feel at ease. 'I thought they would have, but they didn't. The one good thing these experiences have given me has been the opportunity to be here with you. Everything else is meaningless, regrettable in fact.' I told her about the faith's Seven Deadly Sins and the contrasting Seven Heavenly Virtues. The immaturity of youth and a spiritual laziness guided me to the wrong path.

Aanshi said she saw something in me that was waiting to reveal itself. She confidently told me, 'Who you were wasn't who you are or will be.' She took hold of my hand to reassure me of the goodness she saw in my soul. From then on, there was no question of my feelings and future path.

We met every day for months to talk about the beauty around us, our favorite foods, and even gossip a little about the people chaperoning us.   Finally, I brought up the subject of marriage. We had danced around the subject for several weeks as I knew our union would not be one that her family would prefer. To my surprise, she looked at me confidently and gave me a resounding yes for an answer. We knew there were obstacles to overcome.   We had to get the approval of her father and the Portuguese viceroy. I wasn't worried about the viceroy's approval but getting the approval of any father in this type of situation was going to be a challenge.   Commoners usually don't marry princesses.

Aanshi told me to be patient for a few days and to give her time to soften up her father. I waited nearly a week before being called to the court. Wearing my best clothes to give the best impression possible, I had an audience with the Zamorin. Sitting on a luxurious throne and portraying his power as ruler and father, the Zamorin looked me over for a few minutes before beginning the interrogation. 'Captain, it seems you have enchanted my daughter with your tales of the seas. Do you think you are worthy of my most precious jewel?'

'No, your majesty. I am not worthy of her, and I'm not sure I'll ever be. All I can say is that I'll try my best to treat her as the most precious jewel in the world. She means more to me than my own existence. Aanshi has bewitched me, both mind and soul.'

Hearing my response, the Zamorin got the answer that he

wanted and gave us his blessing, 'I would not give such a jewel to a lesser man.' That was a nice compliment. Later, I would find out how strongly he approved of the match because the union would bring a more formidable bond with the Portuguese. I cared little for the political benefits of the union, as long we were allowed to marry.

There was another obstacle that hasn't been mentioned yet. Aanshi had a royal suitor, Ajay, from Calicut who was not happy at the prospect of losing his access to the throne. That bastard Ajay was a real threat, but I was blind to him and the risk he posed to our happiness and lives. We were together and in love, and that's what mattered to us.

In our battle for the soul of the world, the Portuguese had colonial rules that required Aanshi to convert to Catholicism before we could marry. This was also a challenge we had to overcome in Goa. Local women did convert; however, they weren't Zamorin princesses. So, the challenge facing me was far more difficult. While conversions occurred, we allowed the locals to keep their local customs, although years later the inquisition would come to India to stamp out these practices with the converted. To my surprise, the Zamorin did not object, maybe it was due to our allowance of converts to continue observing local customs.

The wedding was the event of the season in Calicut.

Nobility from both Calicut and Portugal came to celebrate the union and to experience an exceptional feast, one they would never forget. The food, the dancing and the exotic rituals were a delight to all the senses. Toward the end of the celebration, the Zamorin pulled me aside for one last piece of fatherly warning. 'I am depending on you to provide a life full of love for my daughter. If you don't, you will be dealing with a very unhappy father-in-law.' He continued speaking in a stern voice, but I tuned him out once I saw Aanshi staring at us. My beautiful bride sensed her father was lecturing me and quickly joined us. After kissing her father's cheek, she grabbed my hand and pulled me onto the dance floor. 'My beloved, you promised me a night of dancing. You can talk to my father later.' The Zamorin tapped his heart, acknowledging his love for his most precious jewel.

Looking back, I told him he would never have to worry as I pledged my life to her. The Zamorin smiled and bowed his head to me. He was satisfied that he made the right choice by approving the marriage.

For the next few years, I captained the new fort built in Calicut, and tried to establish peace and tranquility between the Portuguese and the local population. It wasn't always a successful enterprise, but the spice trade was more profitable than we could have ever imagined. I even had a share in the business. Life was good. Aanshi was my sun, moon and stars. Our life was perfect.

Aanshi gave birth to two of the most beautiful children in creation, first a girl named Lucia and then a boy named Rodrigo. Both were angels sent from heaven who filled our lives with joy each and every day. Lucia had an infectious laugh that could cure the pains of my worst days. I couldn't wait to come home to hear about her daily adventures. Man, what a storyteller she was. Rodrigo was my little fearless warrior who overcame a difficult entrance into the world to become a strong child. He had just started walking when my world came to a crashing end.

Someone was stoking the flames of conflict between the locals and the Portuguese, not that we didn't help the situation. I never suspected it was Ajay and his attempt at revenge for an unrequited love. I had dealt with the bastard with my fists when he called my children cross-bred mongrels during one of the Zamorin's lavish balls. Alcohol makes a nice armor for a coward. I enjoyed giving him a beating he would never forget. He disappeared from court after the Zamorin voiced his displeasure with him as well. No one wants to hear their grandchildren described as mongrels.

Little did I know, Ajay, that pig, was the person who had been enraging the local citizenry about our supposed intention to subjugate them and stamp out their religion. There were incidents where some merchant shops were burned and several ships damaged, however these were rare occurrences. His primary focus of anger was our marriage and how much of an outrage it was to their history and ancestors. It took a few years and some Portuguese errors before Ajay got the mob to focus on us, as well.

That fateful day started with a beautiful sunrise that Aanshi and I shared under its warm glow. I would be busy most of the day completing my monthly inspections of the fort's defenses and armory. Normally, I would come home for lunch, but not this day. Those bloodthirsty snakes must have known. At mid-day, alarms bells were ringing to alert us about a fire along the coast. Looking in the direction of the fire, I noticed that it was near my home. I grabbed my horse and galloped out of the fort like the devil was chasing me. Horrified and panicked, my worst fears were realized. My home was burning.

Rushing inside through the flames, I screamed for Aanshi and the children. Panicking, I ran to each room not caring about the flames burning my flesh. Finally, I was able to locate them. They were all together in our bedroom, huddled together and dead. The smoke and flames had extinguished their lives. Standing motionless and staring at them hopelessly, I screamed to God, asking why this happened. Why did He allow this to happen to three pure souls? I railed against God and his absenteeism. Where was He when my family needed him? Rage and fury filled my heart.

It was then I noticed something clenched in Aanshi's hand. It was a jeweled charm that I had seen before. But where? I struggled to recall where I had seen it. Images quickly flashed through my mind. Was it at the fort, no? At the merchant shops, no? Court, yes? It was Ajay's charm. He wore it the night I beat him. Aanshi must have pulled it from his neck during a fight to protect the children and her home. She knew who did this! My fury grew. With my last breath before I was consumed by the smoke and flames, I cursed the world.

Falling to the floor, dead to the world, the voice of our mutual friend visited me. He offered me a choice to avenge my family and to punish those who committed this most horrible crime. The answer was simple. I succumbed quickly to his enticements and became one of the fallen. I rose from the fiery floor and jumped off the balcony into the sea below without anyone noticing. I rested at the depths of the bay for a short period of time, thinking about Ajay's treachery and continuing to feed my anger. After swimming for a short distance, I walked up to a sandy beach, feeling the immense power the beast had infused in me. I looked different now as well, just as you do, a modern-day Hercules ready for action. You laugh, I know there's some exaggeration on my part. Now, it was time to dispense justice.

After mourning my beloved family for a few days and gathering my strength, my search for Ajay and his co-conspirators began. After about a week, I found the group preparing to burn down another merchant shop. They had been scoping out locations to display their pyrotechnic talents again along the waterfront.

Guessing a Portuguese merchant shop would be their target, I tried to be one step ahead of them. Lying in wait like a lion on the African plains, I hid in the shadows and watching for my victims' arrival. There were five of them, including Ajay. These vandals carried torches and clubs with them to help them complete their cowardly act. Before they could enact their plan and burn down the shop, I stepped out of the shadows and the real fun began.

Those murderous weasels were dispatched with a rage the world had never seen. Stoking the fires of hell, I hacked and tore the heads off each man before they could scream. Blood splattered everywhere. Limbs flying in every direction. I saved the best punishment for Ajay, who fell to his knees crying like a baby. He pleaded for mercy. I asked him why he deserved mercy, and whether he know why he was being punished. At that point, I grabbed his hand and showed my family burning to death as he stood outside my home witnessing their ordeal without emotion. He continued to cry like the coward that he was before I terminated his existence. With one thrust to his chest, I wrenched out his heart as he had done to me and stuffed down his throat.

I haven't looked back since that day. The world is full of evil, and I keep hell's fires burning. It's been a fair arrangement. A conscience is not required for this job. Don't believe those who think that loving your neighbor is what you need to do. I know all about them, they tried that angle with me. Look where it got my beautiful family.

We exist because the world is evil. There are others like us, but most don't survive. Remember when your head was about to split in two. They couldn't handle the anger and desire for vengeance. They just exploded, spontaneous combustion. Poof. We didn't create evil, although sometimes I do wonder if we have had a hand in fertilizing it, making it grow. Are we the chicken or the egg?

The Fisherlady crew is here to help me, it's been part of their punishment to work off their sins for eternity. You've met Ajay already on the boat. He will never repay his debt. I have judged each one of them. Indeed, the judged make very agreeable workers, and they don't need a paycheck.

Tres is here to be my guardian and companion. Hell's gift to me although she's tough on the outside and a marshmallow on the inside. Sometimes, I think she is not well suited for the job, but I love her more than anything.

When Captain Joao finished his story, I just sat across from him, stunned by his tale and how it connected with me. After a few uncomfortable minutes, I found enough strength to respond to him. "Why didn't you fight harder for your own soul?

"Jo-Jo, there's more to my story, our story, that you need to hear. You need to understand who we are and what powers you have!"

Confused and upset, I ran out of the house, grabbing the keys to Angela with Tres following quickly behind me. My destination was Dad and Yo-Yo, a connection to my past, something that would recenter me and to remind me who I was, but I needed to calm down first. Did Captain and I agree to the same bargain? Was this the choice I made? Everything the Captain said pointed to an answer of yes, but I just didn't see it yet. Did my old unbending teenage sensibilities prevent me from seeing the truth?

I drove around town, ultimately stopping at the shore to gaze out over the ocean and to contemplate what Captain's story meant for me. An acceptable answer didn't come to me, only confusion, dread and more questions. The sea was calm that day, a direct contradiction to my emotional state. I contemplated the intentions of these competing forces that wanted me to fulfill my destiny and to begin taking the necessary steps to achieve it. Was it the hand of providence of perdition? What was my destiny? What am I now? Or have I just gone crazy, stuck in a nightmare in an insane asylum under the care of a mad scientist? Questions raged within me as I stared across the sea looking for an answer. I didn't ask for this, but why was I chosen. Was my pain the answer? Was there a remedy?

CHAPTER 15

By this time, it was after 2:30. School would be out for the day, and I had an idea where Yo-Yo would be. Often after school, we would go to Daisy's Ice Cream Shoppe for a frappe. For the novices in the audience, a frappe is a milk shake with ice cream. A milk shake is just a milk shake in Massachusetts, no ice cream, but I digress. Double fudge chocolate was the choice for Yo-Yo and vanilla for me. Don't laugh, but unlike my grandfather, I'm the epitome of vanilla ice cream, boring and average, or I used to be.

Fortunate to find a spot out front, I ordered Tres to stay in the car. The top was down, and we would have a good line of sight to each other. Entering Daisy's, I saw Yo-Yo sitting at the counter with a couple of her girlfriends, ones that I recall from my prior life. They were cackling like normal teenagers about some guy one of the girls thought was cute. Yo-Yo was present in physical form, yet distant at the same time. She seemed lost in a daydream. Trying to be cool, I casually walked over to her.

"Hey, Yo-Yo, right? Funny meeting you here."

Yo-Yo perked right up. "Hi, Isaac. I've been waiting for you. I saved you a seat next to me." She tapped the empty stool to her right.

"You've been waiting for me? How did you know I would be here today?" Fearful that Yo-Yo knew more about me than she should have, I cautiously sat down next to her

"Yes, a little bird told me you were going to come by. It took you long enough."

"Wait a minute. What bird? How would I know you would be here too?" My nervousness was evident to the amusement of Yo-Yo's friends.

The two girls sitting next to her looked at me with delight. "Yup, she's been saying all week that a tall handsome stranger was going to meet her here. We thought she was kidding. Go figure. Say, do you have a bug in your pants?" More teenage giggling ensued.

Awkwardly standing next to Yo-Yo, I could only shake my head in disbelief. "Well, thanks for the compliment."

"Yo-Yo, we must dash. Have fun with Mr. Dreamboat." With a wink and a smile, they giggled as they walked out of the shop. Not being able to contain themselves, the giggling grew louder. Evidently, they were quite a theatrical pair. I don't think

I'd heard the expression "we must dash" before. Her response was typical Yo-Yo, "Moustache to you too."

I sat down next to Yo-Yo in the seat she saved for me, so that we could resume our conversation. "So, you knew I would be here, huh?"

Yo-Yo twirled the straw in her frappe and pondered a response. "Yes, there's something about you that's so familiar. I haven't felt this happy for over three years."

I fidgeted with napkin dispenser on the counter and played it cool. "Since your brother went missing?"

She spun herself around on the counter stool as she had so many times before, and in a clear and calm voice, said something that unnerved me. "Yes, since he went missing. I wonder, though, if he knows how special he is."

"Knows?" My anxiety grew exponentially. No longer playing it cool, I accidentally crushed the napkin dispenser. "Oops. Oh no. Sorry. It seems that I don't know my own strength." A nervous laugh and another apology were all I could muster before fixing the shop's mangled property.

With a firm voice and her eyes locked onto me, she declared, "Yes, and yes, you don't know your own strength."

I didn't know how to respond, other than changing the

subject and ordering my own frappe from an attendant behind the counter. "Can I have a large double thick vanilla frappe. Thank you." I turned my attention back to my sister. "Yo-Yo, tell me about yourself. Are you happy? What do you like to do for fun?"

The last question was the opening she wanted. "I like to paint, mainly portraits. I'm happy seeing how a person develops on my canvas. It feels like we have an unbreakable bond for that short period of time. Will you sit for me?"

"Ahh, sure. When?"

"Now! You drive. I have all my materials at home." Yo-Yo grabbed my hand and pulled me to the door. "C'mon, let's go."

Naturally, I gave into her demands. "OK, I'm coming, but please let me pay for the frappes first."

My beautiful sister could always make me do anything she wanted. Answering *no* was never an option. The joy of that moment was indescribable.

Once we got to the car, Tres was in a state of unbridled frenzy at seeing us. The poor girl couldn't contain her enthusiasm, giving Yo-Yo a bevy of kisses, too numerous to count. We took the short drive over to the house. All the way there, I could see Yo-Yo gleaming in the glow of a warm October day, her face up to the sunlight and smiling from ear to ear. She began to hum a tune that reflected the happiness she was feeling. The tune was the one Mom always hummed when she was happy. It warmed my heart to see and hear these signs of joy. Bliss is a better word for the feeling.

Before we arrived at the house, I could feel Yo-Yo staring at me as she did the other day. "Isaac, it's so odd that you and Jo-Jo both like large double thick vanilla frappes. Don't you think?"

I still tried to play it cool. "No, it just means he has really good taste."

When we arrived at the house, Yo-Yo bounded up the back stairs. She asked me to sit in the yard with Tres while she got her art supplies. It appeared that no one else was home. Dad must be delayed with a problem at work. Glad to see nothing's changed there. I took note of the negative feelings rising within me concerning my dad and tried to suppress them. My focus had to be on Yo-Yo.

Tres and I made our way to the patio in the backyard. The space was configured with eye-catching splendor, as if it came out of a home improvement magazine. It had an outdoor kitchen, pizza oven, hideaway television and entertainment center, and an eight-person spa. Did I suddenly get transported to LA? My parents would never have installed something as extravagant as this. This was all Kat's doing.

I sat on one of the couches waiting patiently for her to join me. Yo-Yo quickly returned and set up her art supplies: graphite pencils, erasers and large drawing paper. Tres immediately jumped on her to give her another rounded of kisses. "No paint today?"

Yo-Yo arranged her art supplies on a coffee table in front of me. "Nah, just thinking of drawing both of you together today. Please sit close to each other on the couch."

"Won't your mom be upset about Tres on the couch?"

Yo-Yo snapped back quickly, "Kat is not my mom, not even close! My mom's in heaven with the angels."

"Oh, sorry. I didn't mean to upset you." Her reaction was perfect. I was glad to see she wasn't fooled by Kat's game.

Yo-Yo alternatively looked at her sheet and me with one squinted eye and head tilted. She had the artistic flair of an old pro. "No worries. Now, just sit still. No fidgeting around."

"Yes, ma'am." I made sure to salute her.

Yo-Yo drew for about 30 minutes, ripping up pages intermittently that didn't meet her standards or her vision of me. Finally, she looked at her final piece and nodded with approval. "All done. Tuh-Dah!" She couldn't contain her emotions and the confidence she felt in capturing our essence.

Brimming with youthful enthusiasm and excitement, she revealed her completed drawing. Like a bolt of lightning hitting me, I was struck by her perception of us. Yo-Yo saw me as she had in our prior sessions, except darker and sadder. While I didn't look like Jo-Jo, it had the same look and feel. Tres, on the other hand, was drawn beautifully, head leaning, tongue hanging out and smiling.

"Wow. It's beautiful, and a little haunting for one of us. Do you really see me this way?"

"Yup. There is something about you, Isaac, that reminds me of my brother. You both have this same serious and brooding exterior that's just a cover for someone who thinks he's lost but doesn't know why. Maybe, it's the way you see the world negatively, or how you think the world sees you. Jo-Jo was always stuck in a dark place, emerging every so often to try to experience something happy. He was his own worst critic, but I see you both as goofy, sad, and withdrawn! That's how you look to me, withdrawn." Yo-Yo began to giggle uncomfortably at her pun. My sister could still read me, whatever my form. Regardless, I was stunned and was speechless.

Yo-Yo chimed back, "Oh, don't worry big fella. I have faith that you'll find your way out of the dark." Once again, her inner light was shining, showing me how special she was. Mom would have been proud.

At that point, while still stunned and before I could dig deeper into her comments, Dad and Kat pulled into the driveway, along with Decker, Riley and Jenny. They walked into the backyard talking over each other about the opening of the pub tomorrow night. All, save Jenny, were full of excitement, until, that is, Decker and Riley saw me. Walking behind everyone, Jenny was quiet and emotionless. She had fallen deeper into her own abyss and was clearly at a point of unmitigated despair. I took notice right away. Back on mission!

Kat was first to talk, naturally. "Hey JR, Isaac's here for another visit. Looks like he's been modelling for Yo-Yo. Isaac, this is my son, Decker. You didn't get a chance to meet him the other day."

My dad extended his hand to greet me. "Hey, I'm glad you could come over today. Apologies for not being here earlier but I forgot about the tour of the renovated pub today. It looks awesome. Decker, what's it called, a gastropub?"

Placing his arm around my dad's shoulders, Decker responded with air of conceit and self-assurance. "Yes, that's it, a place for good beer, good drinks and good food. We will be the hottest spot on the North Shore." Random thought, his arm needs to be broken soon!

"Wow, that sounds great. I'm going to have to stop by tomorrow. What's the name?" I noticed Decker looked uncomfortable and shuffled his feet in place upon hearing my desire to attend the opening.

Riley answered for Decker, "It's called Trips." His response was delivered with little intonation and was noticeably cold. Like Decker, he was obviously bothered by my presence. "Mom, can we eat now. I'm starving." Interesting, Riley called Kat, mom. Was she the matriarch of the whole Mannion clan or was it a son-in-law sucking-up to the in-laws? Who knew, and I didn't care.

"Sure, baby, we're going to have to order takeout or delivery. I didn't have time to prepare anything. Isaac, you can join us if you want."

Obviously, I wasn't really welcome there, even though I wanted to probe this trio of miscreants a little more. Jenny flashed a gentle and momentary smile at me, a type of smile that continued to solidify my doubts on her complicity in the whole affair. Riley, however, caught Jenny and wasn't too happy. With fiery eyes and a stern countenance, his expression was malevolent and jealous.

I sensed my presence would cause an immediate problem for Jenny and possibly for my plan. Backing away and waving, I thanked them for the invitation. "My sincere apologies, but I have to be on the boat early tomorrow. We haven't been out for a few days because of the repairs, and Captain is keen on hitting his target catch total before winter. Goodnight, and good luck tomorrow night."

Trying to get Tres away from Yo-Yo took a few minutes, as they had seemingly become bonded. Walking slowly to the car, I could hear Decker and Riley talking about me. Did I tell you I have super-power hearing now? These two miscreants were discussing how they didn't like me. Apparently, one of Riley's friends saw Jenny with me at the coffee shoppe. I dropped my keys in the driveway to allow for more time to listen to their discussion.

Decker was firm in his perspective on the matter. "T-Rex told me he saw Jenny and this guy having coffee together the other day, and they were looking very cozy. He said it looked they were on a date. Now, I trust my sister, but this guy is crossing the line. Riley, what are you, or we, going to do about it? I don't like this guy popping up lately. Who is he?"

"And she was out for most of the day yesterday," Riley grumbled. "Don't like him. I think he needs to go on a boat trip."

Decker's eyes remained focused on me, his new prey. "Agreed. I'll round up T-Rex for a little mischief on the boat."

What this meant for Jenny wasn't clear, but a blind man could see it wasn't going to be good for me. The bait had been taken. Turning back to them, I flashed a smile along with a friendly wave. Looking innocent and appearing oblivious to the developing battle was critical at this point. As for T-Rex? It's great to have him involved in this, one less step for me.

On the way home, I stopped for a celebratory meal at another of my favorite sandwich places. There's nothing more satisfying than a 'super-beef-three-way' with steak fries and a pizza roll after a long, successful day. A sandwich piled high with warm rare roast beef on an onion roll with American cheese, barbeque sauce and mayonnaise. Of course, there was a cheeseburger for Tres too. We ate down at the waterfront, sitting on a bench and watching the boats navigate past us, up and down the channel. It was a good day, but Jenny still was a puzzle to me, and Yo-Yo's drawing haunted me still. What was she trying to say? Did she know more? The more I thought about it, the more it occurred to me that she was as pure and powerful as our mom. She had a power that I could never understand, as if heaven existed on earth, shining a light for those dwelling in darkness and despair.

Early the next morning, Captain rustled me out of bed. "Hey, we're fishing today. Maybe catch a blue fin or two. Vamos. Let's go. We have a lot to discuss too." Not moving fast enough for his liking, Captain ripped the covers off me and kicked the bed frame to make sure I got the point.

It was obvious that we were going out, not to catch fish, but to discuss Captain's revelation from the prior day. Angling for blue fin was an excuse to keep me under control and to get me on the Fisherlady. Or perhaps, I was the catch of the day, ready to be plated. We would soon discover the status of our relationship as individuals, specters, or whatever we were.

The dock was especially busy that day. All the boat Captains wanted to take advantage of the mild weather and calm seas before another indefinable New England winter. As much as we loved them, New England winters always provided several months of challenges and pain, both expected and unexpected, but these annual tests made people more resilient and less averse to severe weather. Who else would wear shorts in 40-degree weather without thinking twice?

All the captains and their crew would yell out the same greeting of good fortune to each other, "Tight lines and a bent rod." You never, never tell a fisherman *good luck* unless you want a salty response or a black eye. The movement on the docks was frenetic, a choreographed dance, as the crews worked to store their daily supplies of food, drink and bait on their boats. It was Broadway on the Docks.

We loaded our gear onto the Fisherlady's deck quickly. Captain didn't want to delay getting out of the harbor and addressing today's two objectives, catching fish and convincing me to fully accept my fate. I played along, whistling an old sailor's tune while we pulled away from the dock. We made our way out to Georges Bank, a prime blue fin fishing location, to start our day.

Captain walked up beside me as I sat on the aftdeck contemplating my path and watching several baited reels that had already been cast into the ocean. "Captain, why do you fish? It's not like you need money."

"Of course, I need money. I'm not a magician who can create money out of thin air, although alchemy powers do sound great. Being able to turn lead into gold would be fantastic." An odd blank expression came to Captain's face, as he pondered how great it would be to have that as a supernatural power. "Remember, we are part of this world and the next, half in one and half in the other. We have a physical body that needs nourishment, all kinds of nourishment." Captain's belly laugh echoed across the deck.

Nothing worse than an old guy making sexual references. I rubbed my stomach to show my physical revulsion to his comment. "OK, that last part sounds sick and creepy."

"No, seriously, our bodies are living in two worlds and have been given powers from each. To do the job we need to do, we must be able to understand these powers. There is so much you need to know. You are stronger now than any human being in the world. You and I have been granted an ability to attract and trap those bastards and scoundrels that need to be judged. And our verdicts are final. Remember the aroma of cinnamon rolls. We have several other lures. You just need to know when to use the right one. Have you tried your super-hearing yet, or your ability to sense danger brewing?"

His revelation intrigued me. I leaned in closer to him, looking to know more. "Yes, I've experienced these powers. What else can you tell me?"

"Well, that's just the tip of the iceberg." He paused for a moment to allow me to reflect on what was revealed so far.

I sat motionless contemplating and trying to prepare my response. "Have you ever transported an offender, the judged as you call them, to a place where they see and feel the results of their actions, their sins? It was terrifying."

Captain smiled with satisfaction, happy that my powers had progressed so well. "Yes, that is a power that only a rare few of our kind have. You are special to have it."

Each revelation made me feel special, like I was part of an extraordinary team who had a heavenly purpose. "Do you have it?"

"Yes, but there are other amazing powers that are lying just beneath the surface and waiting to be revealed. You will need these for the battles ahead. I'm sorry about unloading my story onto you yesterday, but you needed to hear it. Reaching full potential has always been a solitary journey for our kind. That's why only a select few can handle the gift while others just implode, but I see something very special in you that I cannot describe. I am here to be your guide, a sort of captain to first mate relationship on an old Man O' War."

"Easy big fella. I like you, but not that much." My laughter was punctuated with a more serious tone and question. "Captain, please tell me what we are? I need to know." I pleaded for an answer.

Captain leaned back and heaved a reflective sigh. "Well, Jo-Jo, I imagine you have some idea based on your recent experiences. Fundamentally, we are judges, here to punish the wicked and feed them to the fires of hell. We are part messenger from the afterlife and part human who pronounce judgment on the wicked swiftly and without remorse. How did you feel when you were evaluating that person and showing him his true self, his wickedness?"

"Odd to say, alive, like my life, or existence, had a purpose."

"Good. Fantastic. The original judges, or as I prefer to call us, wraiths, were created thousands of years ago to keep the repentant faithful and in God's good grace, but the world grew more disgusting and vile along with humanity's intellectual appetite as the years passed. With increasing innovation, people found new ways to fall from grace. I did, that's for sure. Freedom of will is the greatest gift bestowed on humankind, but most don't deserve it. We couldn't handle the expansion of our minds and our potential without falling from grace. Our calling changed from caretaker to executioner, once we saw how they could never truly repent. We changed with the passing millennia, meeting evil with increasing ruthlessness. Falling further from grace themselves and unable to handle the world's increasing darkness, wraiths dwindled in number. They just disappeared, poof, plain and simple. Today, there are very few of us to punish the wicked and feed hell's fires. Today, we are overwhelmed by the weight of our task and the immensity of the darkness that surrounds us. We operate in darkness now, outside the glow of grace, because that's what humanity deserves. Uncle Trick taught me how to operate in the dark and to continue my path through the world. Jo-Jo, you are first one to survive the change in the last 200 years. We need you."

Confused, I raised my hands to my head and paced the deck. "Who is Uncle Trick? Why is this the first time I'm hearing about him? He isn't the...?" I couldn't complete my sentence as a feeling of dread came over me.

"He taught the remaining few wraiths how to cope with the modern world, swiftly and without remorse. He wants to meet you."

A chill ran up my spine. The Great Deceiver wanted to meet me and make me one of the fallen. All I could say was, "I don't know. I just don't know. And what did you mean I was the first to survive the change in the past 200 years? You said, 'they just disappeared.' What happened to them and to their souls? Are they in heaven, hell, or just gone from creation?" These last questions filled me with enormous panic and fear. My pacing across the deck intensified.

Sensing my growing anxiety and a reluctance to accept Uncle Trick, Captain took a different approach at calming me. "Listen, let's take this one topic at a time. Let me show you something cool."

Captain rose, closed his eyes for a moment and began to transform. First, his eyes turned red followed by a strange elongation of his face that looked painful. Slowly, the metamorphosis moved to the rest of his body as his arms, legs and torso turned and twisted in ways not biologically possible. Soon, appearing before me was Death, the Pale Rider, a gaunt yet muscular form standing on two powerful legs, razor sharp fangs of a wild beast and a skin of ashen gray. He had long stringy hair draped over his shoulders, otherwise his body was hairless. I thought I was going to soil myself but then another change came.

"Jo-Jo, watch this." I guess this metamorphosis didn't restrict Captain's ability to speak. Suddenly, a pair of colorfully radiant angel wings burst out of his back. The contrast of his wings and the skin covering his body was disquieting, for it showed Captain as a being living in both light and darkness. I was in awe, my mouth and eyes wide open, and motionless at this terrifying sight. In an instant, Captain leaped from the deck and into the sky, soaring higher with each beat of his wings, and then darting across the boat's stern. It was good there were no other boats near us to see the spectacle, otherwise our next appearance would have been social media.

Captain then swooped down and hovered over the aftdeck. "Jo-Jo, this is you power too. Close your eyes and submit yourself to the transformation. You've experienced some of this before, didn't you? Now, you just need to accept it."

Standing silently on the deck and contemplating his request, I considered my options. Do I grab the brass ring or jump back into the sea? My decision was quick; I still had a job to do. The Trinity of Evil still needed to pay the butcher's bill. I accepted my fate and focused on my transformation into a beastly creation, wings and all. Power surged through me, morphing my body with each audible crack and rumble. At first, it felt like my skin, bones and limbs were being torn apart. The pain was excruciating. I screamed to Captain for help, but he did not come. Suddenly, straddling both light and darkness, an unexpected feeling of harmony came to me. In an instant, my metamorphosis was complete, and it was fantastic.

Leaping into the sky, I felt like a butterfly awkwardly emerging from its cocoon. Tres frantically bounded around the deck and barked her approval. After a few minutes, I was able to control my path. Captain couldn't contain his joy and joined me on my maiden flight. Soaring through the clouds at breakneck speed, a feeling of exhilaration pulsated through my body. I never felt more alive. Growing more confident in my abilities, I decided that the time had come to bring my wrath upon Decker, Riley, and most of all, Kat.

Captain noticed that two of the lines had hooked fish. "Hey, we got a bite. Let's get back, quick."

We dove back onto the aftdeck and changed immediately back to our human form with merely a thought. We pulled in two beautiful blue fin cows that had to weigh over 500 pounds each. It was going to be a nice pay day for us.

"Now that's what I'm talking about. I knew you were my good luck charm. Obrigado, Isaac! Let's go home and celebrate the fruit of labor."

Marking a somber tone, I advised Captain of my other plans. "Sorry, I can't tonight. There's somewhere I need to be. Tonight, it's opening night at the pub."

"Well then, you better get to it. There will be more lessons tomorrow. Now, help me pack these cows with ice so they don't spoil."

A few hours later, Captain dropped me off at home for a quick shower while he went out for a celebratory meal. I was ready for what was to come, but I also knew the three miscreants were not. Tonight, the finishing touches to the first part of my plan would be completed and judgement would soon come to Decker, Riley and T-Rex. The reflection in the mirror agreed with me.

Arriving there fashionably late, I looked around the bar area for a familiar face. Almost immediately, Yo-Yo jumped in front of me in a failed attempt to startle me. Remember, one of my powers is the ability to sense danger. "Boo. Gotcha. Where were you? You're late." Her eyes sparkled against the lights of the neon bar signs as she gave me the biggest hug she could.

Not wanting to let go of her, I laughed. "Sorry, I had a busy day on the boat today. You wouldn't want me to show up smelling of fish and low tide, would you?"

Finally, releasing me from her bear hug, Yo-Yo roared her approval. "Thanks, I don't like hugging fish, maybe a puppy though. Where's Tres?"

"No Tres tonight. She was a busy girl today. She's at home resting."

Dad, Kat and Jenny walked up behind Yo-Yo to greet me.

Dad welcomed me first, "Hey, Isaac. Thanks for coming. Hey Kat. Isaac's here."

"JR, I can see him. Hey, Isaac. Great to see you could join us tonight." While she spoke, Kat had an odd expression, sort of like she was thinking more negatively about my presence and possible motives. I would soon get a clue as to why.

Dad moved the conversation to my fishing exploits. "Were the fish biting today?"

"Yup, we caught two 500-pound blue fins. It's been a really good day. Hey Jenny, how are you?"

Jenny stared at me looking lost again, but this time I noticed a bruise on her arm. "What happened to your arm? Looks painful." My superpower radar was on high alert.

Jenny responded in a less than convincing tone, "Ahhh. Oh. I slipped last night in the shower. I can be such a klutz sometimes."

Obviously, she was lying, covering up for Riley's physical abuse, but why wouldn't Kat or Dad take notice of this. Perhaps, they didn't want to notice or care. Then again, my father was clueless to these sorts of things. Kat, on the other hand, had to know, and as such, a possible explanation to her earlier scrutinizing gaze directed toward me. There's trouble in paradise and I'm at the center of it. Perfect.

We sat at the end of the bar, drinking one of the local IPAs, except for Yo-Yo drinking a ginger-ale. The conversation meandered from topic to topic but always returned to how great the boys did with the bar and how special they were to Kat. I wanted to vomit – both spiritually and physically – listening to Kat's voice.

Soon, the boys and T-Rex came over to say hello as the rest of the group dispersed across the pub to talk to friends. The four of us were alone now.

Decker was first to talk. "Hey, Bro', how's it going? Thanks for coming." Nice try, Bro'. What an idiot! It was easy to see through his artificially sweetened good humor. Riley stood behind him, stewing with his jaw clenched tight. "Have you met our buddy, T-Rex? He's an old friend of Jenny too. They went to college together."

T-Rex grunted his greeting like any respectable neanderthal would. "Hey Bro'. What's up?"

I decided to have some fun. "T-Rex. Nice to meet you. Didn't you know Jonah when Jenny dated him in college?"

His reaction was perfect. His body began to quiver as he digested my question. His voice quaked slightly as he stammered through a response. "No. No. N-Never met Jo-Jo. Jenny was always a private girl in college. She didn't like to broadcast her personal life. Still doesn't."

He didn't realize I had asked about someone named Jonah and not Jo-Jo. So, it seems he was involved in my demise as well. "That's too bad. I would like to have heard more about him. It's very sad to hear he's been missing for a few years now." T-Rex remained incapacitated by the fear introduced by my question.

Here was the opening Decker was looking for. He took the bait. "Riley and I can tell you about Jo-Jo. He was a good kid, very quiet."

By this time, I had clasped my hands behind my back to present an image of naivete. They needed to see me as innocent and harmless. "He *was* a good kid? I thought he was missing. Did something happen to him?"

Realizing he slipped up, Decker stammered with a response, "Y-yes, he is still missing. After all these years, I often think he has passed on, but he's never forgotten. We can tell you more about Jo-Jo if you are interested. How about joining us out on the boat tomorrow so that we can chat more? We would like to get to know you better too. JR thinks you're the best thing since sliced bread. Maybe you can give us some pointers on catching blue fins?"

So, it appears these three miscreants are using the old tried and true approach of getting their victim out to sea and away from prying eyes, where there would be no witnesses, no body, and no crime. The unsuspecting fools were in for a surprise, a fatal one, in fact.

"JR is way too generous with his compliments. The boat trip does sound like a great idea. I'm a bit-tired tonight, so I'm going to bale. It would be nice to get a good night's rest after a hard day's work."

"Great! We're closing soon. Since this is only a soft opening, we are shutting down early too. Meet us at the dock tomorrow at seven unless you're working."

"No, I'm not working." Captain wouldn't begrudge giving me the day off once I told him the particulars of my upcoming sea excursion. "Captain has business out of town. I can meet you at the dock, since I have to drop some gear at the Fisherlady anyway for our next trip."

We all agreed on the plan and parted for the evening. Riley remained motionless, seemingly ready to spontaneously combust, while assaulting me with his cold and soulless eyes. Understanding the danger of the situation, I could see Riley was visualizing my demise step by step and blow by blow. Each taking their turn clubbing me, while the others laughed. Oh, the excruciating pain they are going to feel tomorrow!

Later that evening, Captain and I reviewed my plan in depth, hashing out what to expect and how to use my powers. Captain revealed another power to me, the power of invisibility or to be seen only by certain people. After describing how to deploy it, Captain had me practice a few times on unsuspecting neighbors when I took Tres out for a late evening walk. With Tres beside me off leash, I made myself completely invisible first or then visible only to certain people. It worked perfectly. When I was completely invisible, all the neighbors' comments were directed to Tres. "Hey girl, did you get out of the yard?" No one was afraid of Tres, as scary as she could be, because everyone knew and loved her. We just kept walking. When I was partially invisible, the reactions were better, almost comical. The one or two people who could see me would say hi, while the others who couldn't see me, would look at their walking partners with confusion, "Who are you talking to?"

Ultimately, Captain counseled me to avoid getting too cute with my maneuverings and just get the job done without being seen. Cell phone cameras were everywhere nowadays and were always a concern for him, but he agreed to stay away from the dock and not interfere. It was time for this baby bird to leave the nest for a solo flight.

CHAPTER 16

The trio of miscreants met me at the Fisherlady at 7:00 on the nose. I had gotten there 15 minutes earlier to give the appearance that the boat was being stocked for the next trip, packing snacks in the galley and nonsensically moving gear from side to side and back again. I made sure I was seen by the other crews.

Being the vocal ambassador for the group, Riley was first to speak. "Hey, Isaac. What's going on?"

Trying to appear focused on my boat preparation activities, I jumped up, looking surprised. "Hey! Geez. You guys scared me." My acting performance was award worthy, if I do say so myself. Appearing to settle down after the shock, I patted my chest and continued with my tasks. "How you guys doing today? Everything go OK last night after I left?"

Placing one foot on the Fisherlady deck, Riley appeared innocent and calm. "All good. We had a decent crowd for opening night. Are you ready to go?"

Taking care of my final fake task, I was ready to go. "Yup. Just need to lock the door to the cabin and I'm done. Let's roll."

Riley's demeanor turned cold. He clenched his jaw and stared at me menacingly, while the other two stood on the dock grinning. "Great. Leave your car here. Our boat is docked close-by. We can walk."

I made myself visible only to the three miscreants. Just in case there were witnesses in the yard still, I would have an alibi. Decker and T-Rex looked around the waterfront, presumably to also assess whether there was anyone around who could have witnessed their presence on the dock and potentially invalidate their account with investigators. I often wondered how they avoided suspicion three years earlier, but that didn't matter today.

During the short walk over to their boat, I pondered whether I was making this too complicated. Just execute them one by one and that's it. Walking behind Riley and Decker, I could reach over to T-Rex and rip out his throat, then eviscerate Decker. Riley would be last due to the pain he inflicted on Jenny, as evidenced by her black and blue arm. Vibrant scenes of mayhem, bedlam and men sinking into a pool of blood played out repeatedly in my mind. Although it brought a smile to my face, I decided to make it a group execution on the boat, where privacy could afford me more time to torment this trio of miscreants.

My forthcoming neanderthal quarry, T-Rex, was eyeing me

during the walk to their boat. "Bro' are you ok? What are you smiling at?"

"Nothing, T-Rex, nothing at all." I was feeling good about what was about to happen, and it was going to be epic.

While puzzled, T-Rex decided to end the conversation as we arrived at their boat. The boat looked the same as that fateful day three years ago. I stopped to look it over from stem to stern. Memories of my execution three years earlier rushed back to me, but I needed to play it cool. "Nice boat. She's a beauty. Nice name too, Tesoro. It means Treasure, doesn't it?"

Riley, being especially proud of the boat, expressed his thanks. "Yes, it does. Let's get on and push off. It's going to be a nice day, and we don't want to miss any part of it."

We pulled away from the dock and motored out of the harbor and into open waters. I sat on a chair placed for me on the stern as the three miscreants whispered together. Thinking that they were safely out of hearing range, they went over their plan to murder me. They knew or heavily suspected that Jenny and I were intimate. For that, Riley wanted me to pay a fatal price quickly, no more waiting. About an hour or so into our journey and far from prying eyes, they emerged from the cabin to confront me. I remained seated and motionless, with my eyes closed and basking in the sun's rays.

Decker initiated the festivities. "Hey, Isaac, do you know the story of the boy who got caught sticking his hand in the cookie jar? It's a story of greed and theft, sort of like what you've done with Jenny. What do you have to say for yourself?"

Unaffected by his taunts, I remained completely still and gave no indication of fear or concern.

Decker became agitated. "Bro' what's wrong with you? Did you hear me? This guy is a freakin' weirdo." My lack of reaction infuriated him more. "Seriously, did you escape from the looney farm?"

T-Rex laughingly added his two cents. "I think this dude definitely has a few screws loose. Can we just finish the job before this nut job gets weirder?"

Suddenly, Riley rushed forward with a bat and hit me across my shoulders with such speed and ferocity that it splintered into hundreds of pieces. Riley looked at his broken weapon of murder in shock. "What the..!"

Slowly and deliberately, I rose from my chair and told these boys a tale they would never forget. "Gentlemen, it's time for me to tell you a story. Have you heard the one about a boy who loved a girl, but this girl was born into an inbred family of criminals and morons?" I could feel their fear growing now and it was intoxicating. "This family brought a boy on a trip to murder him, because their whore of a mother wanted revenge, misguided as it was, for a brother who committed suicide many years earlier. Now, this family has been living in the past for its entire existence. This footing in the past only resulted in the family's stunted growth and an inability to build or even conceive a normal future. Be wary of people held captive by the past because they are only good at sowing sorrow." I became a little philosophical at the end of my speech. It couldn't be helped, I was feeling a bit righteous, and these morons needed to be taught a verbal lesson before judgement was rendered.

With a bellowing howl, the Pale Rider emerged as the boys fell to their knees, crying in panic and paralyzed by sheer terror. "Crying and pleas of mercy will not help you. Judgment day is here boys and Jo-Jo says hi, but first, you all need to suffer the pain of your sins before I send you to hell's fires."

All three continued to beg; they understood the shocking revelation raised with Jo-Jo's name. T-Rex and Riley attempted to jump overboard for an improbable escape, but I easily prevented their premature leap into oblivion by releasing my wings and capturing them in mid-jump. Knocking them out, I turned my attention to Decker.

"Decker, time to feel the pain of your sins." I took hold of his arms and Decker relived his sins, all of them, including torturing animals, stealing, and participating in my prior demise.

He was laughing the fateful day three years ago but not today. Then, something even more heinous was revealed to me as we watched his sins. Decker had been molesting Jenny since she was a teenager and nearly up to the time she met me, when I was still Jo-Jo. I saw nights when Decker would sneak into her room and force himself on her. After he completed his carnal pleasures, Jenny would curl up into a fetal position staring into oblivion and trying to forget her trauma, to lock it away, far away. It was the same after each rape. After each monstrous night, Decker would say how much he loved her and that no one could love her as much as he could. This family was worse than I thought. Kat had raised an individual of pure evil. My heart ached for Jenny and the pain she carried. My rage reached a level of spontaneous combustion, almost nuclear. "You bastard! What did you? What did you do?"

It was this time for a trip to perdition. Decker screamed the most awful sounds I had ever heard. He promised me that he would be good man going forward and to even be my helper. I couldn't listen to his sniveling and cries for mercy. Placing my hand over his heart and holding it there until his life ended in a slow painful death, I sent him to damnation. "Go to hell and burn!"

Next, I woke up Riley by slapping his face, harder than necessary but still justified. "Riley, wake up little piggie."

Riley opened his eyes, startled and incapacitated by fear. "Please stop. I haven't done anything. Please."

"Stop crying. You can't even admit what you've done with the life that you've led and the pain you've caused. No remorse? I was there that day you killed Jo-Jo, wasting both of your lives."

"No, please. I only did what I was told to do. He was a danger to the family, and we had to protect ourselves."

The nature of the battle came more into focus for me. My rage, some may call it righteous anger, became clear to Riley. I couldn't hold back thoughts that had been reverberating through my mind. I had been formulating a personal philosophy and had to shout it out loud. Like water bursting through a broken dam, I let loose. "Did you say, 'we only did what we were told to do?!' Well, you did what you were told to do. How many times have men of weak character said that? You have a spiritual laziness or slothfulness that the beast loves so well, an apathy toward expanding your knowledge of the world that surrounds you. Did your closed mind create a breeding spot for this fatal flaw to reproduce like weeds in the forest, where a fabricated anxiety was cultivated and drove you farther away from grace? Or was it ignorance of other people's differences, a superficial threat invented by a mind clenched in fear? Or did pride overtake you? Were you so entirely focused on yourself and family that arrogance and vanity dwelled without a second thought? Does your importance outweigh another's?"

I wanted to extend his time on earth; he needed to feel more pain. Perhaps it was more for my benefit, but the lecture continued. "Riley, listen to me. Fear is the bastard child of ignorance and pride, a sin that can sever us from heaven's grace. The beast knows this and so does the wolf, but you chose the beast. What happened to charity, kindness and humility? Would showing any of these be considered a sign of weakness, or make you less of a man? Was it the belief that sins of the father become the sins of the son? You have lived so much in the past that you lost the future, never growing and reaching full potential. You allowed the past to control you and to create your destiny, a life wasted. Free will can become nightmare whenever it's misused. You've lost heaven on earth, for nothing! Your ignorance and vanity made you nothing more than a neanderthal."

Riley pleaded in vain for his life. It was a beautifully pitiful sight to behold. "Please, I don't understand."

"Of course, you don't, moron. You were even blind to Decker's assaults on Jenny. My lecturing is wasted on you." With my pontificating done, I decapitated him with one slash of my hand. I held his head as a trophy over his headless body for him to see. "Hell's waiting for you."

Finally, I shifted my attention to the day's last victim, who was too stupid to bother prolonging his agony. Waking the neanderthal from his slumber, I shared with T-Rex a greeting from his past. "Jo-Jo sends his best wishes, and you're going to need sunscreen where you're going."

T-Rex crumbled into a fetal position and cried like the coward and bully he always was. "Jo-Jo, no! it wasn't me. I swear, it wasn't me." Ripping his heart out was enough justice for this swine. He'll remembering meeting me now.

Having completed the last of my fatal tasks, I prepared the boat to explode. A boating accident caused by a faulty fuel line would be headlines in the local papers. While going through these preparations, images of Jenny being assaulted haunted me. Her agony shot through me and altered my mood like quicksilver. Satisfaction for a job well done turned to an atomic level rage. An even more terrifying and nauseating image reverberated in my mind. It was the image of Kat catching him in the act. She knew about it! Instead of helping her daughter, she helped the agent of the crime, her son. I could see her slapping him and telling him how wrong it was to do what he did. Then, as he sat crying holding onto her, she forgave him. "It's not your fault. You didn't understand what you were doing. Don't worry, Jenny won't say anything. She knows you love her. Plus, she had a part in this too. She didn't look like she minded." Kat then slapped Jenny repeatedly for tempting Decker. "This is what a girl gets with your flirty attitude and little short-shorts." All Jenny could do was to stare without expression and emotion into the far corner of the room where her mom was scolding her.

I paused for a moment to gaze upwards to the beautifully blue sky, and possibly into the heavens. The horror of Jenny's ordeal made me contemplate the purpose of my mission, or existence for that matter. Children were the most precious creation ever entrusted to humanity. What were we if we couldn't protect them? A child who spoke the words "mom or dad" uttered the sweetest sounds ever created. A child was innocence and purity incarnate, the heartbeat of the world. Children were meant to be our future, the best of us, and not doomed to live in a romanticized past that exaggerates the future. We have failed them.

The real enemies of humanity were apathy, ignorance and pride. These have shaped all of our fears, and not an unquenchable curiosity of the unknown. We have allowed ourselves to be driven to unconscionable action or inaction. We weren't born wearing blinders; we put them on ourselves. In my case, fear was paralyzing, a devil's recipe to accept the status quo of an indifferent world. Captain's perspective came into better focus. The world was cruel. There was no hope for it.

After throwing the fruits of my labor into the ocean without a chance of being found, I radioed a distress call with extreme panic in my voice. With that done, I made myself invisible and flew back to the Fisherlady. The flight back was an incredible experience. Flying high and low through the sunny blue sky, racing with seagulls and spying on fishing boats from above, I felt satisfied that the appropriate punishments were delivered to the three. Trips was going to need new management.

Flying over the dock, I could see that Captain Joao was waiting there for me on the Fisherlady, with a giant smile on his face and ready to congratulate me.   He held a 6-pack of our favorite IPA to start the celebration. It was a good day.

Over the next few days, I kept a low profile by working on the boat. News came out about the accident. The Coast Guard searched for days before quitting. The local news showed Kat at the dock crying with my dad holding her tightly. There was no sign of Jenny.

About a week later, a church service was held for the three miscreants.   There were no bodies, so nothing to bury, which provided a little more anguish for Kat. I decided to attend the ceremony, not because I wanted to be a witness to Kat's anguish, but rather to satisfy a need to see Sister Alicia, Mother and Tiny. There was so much I wanted to discuss with them. They had warned me about the path that I was taking. Maybe, my actions were as wrong as the ones being judged. Reaping but never sowing, am I living in the past as well?

At the end of the service, I offered my condolences to Kat and Jenny. Kat was now a broken person being held by my dad and an emotionless Jenny held by Yo-Yo. Kat and dad stopped for a moment and could only nod in my direction. Yo-Yo and Jenny stopped near me and smiled. In unison, they thanked me for coming and asked where had I been lately?

"I stayed away to give your family time to grieve. How are you guys doing?"

From outside the church, Kat yelled, "Jenny. Yo-Yo. We need to go to the dock to lay a wreath for the boys."

Jenny responded in a manner that is best described as monotone and lifeless, "Coming. Isaac, do you want to come with us?"

"Sure. I'll meet you down there. First, I have to talk to three old friends." I replied, pointing to the altar where they were standing. Jenny took notice of Sister Alicia.

"Wow. Sister Alicia. I always liked her even though I was kind of mean to her at times." Her voice was sincere and marked with pangs of guilt. She remembered the juvenile taunts and snarky responses directed at Sister during our days on campus with the BCs. It's amazing how a crowd can increase a person's courage, especially the courage to act like an idiot.

Smiling, Yo-Yo chimed in as they left the church, "We better see you there if you know what's good for you." Yo-Yo could always make me smile, which she did again that day.

Beckoning me to come up to the altar, they waited silently for me to come forward. Next to them, an image of the Virgin

Mary rested in an alcove. On my slow walk up the side aisle toward them, I stopped at this beautiful statue to pray for a moment, as she had always been a source of great comfort and consolation. Although I wasn't particularly religious in my prior life, the Holy Virgin did offer a certain level of solace to me during my lower points, as she kept me from hitting rock bottom. I stood there motionless, lost in time, looking for guidance and silently praying for relief. While the three miscreants had been judged according to their sins, something didn't feel right.

After allowing me a few moments of private contemplation, Sister Alicia and her companions walked over to the alcove, joining me as I finished a short prayer. It was an odd feeling, but their presence relaxed me, even Tiny. "Good morning." I said in a reverent tone.

Sister Alicia, holding her rosary tightly, stopped at my side to greet me. "Good morning, child. How are you today? You look preoccupied."

"I'm OK. It's good to see you. The last time we spoke, I wasn't exactly the best company. Apologies for my rudeness in how the conversation ended."

She seemed to take great comfort in my apology and gently smiled her approval. "Thank you, child. You know it will take a lot more to upset me, but I was disappointed."

At that last comment, something in me moved and fixated on the essence of my soul. I dropped again to my knees in front of the Virgin and cried softly. "I don't know who or what I am anymore. I should be happy, but I'm not. There's no need to ask whether you knew what I did last week."

Sister Alicia placed her hand on my back to comfort me. "We know. How did it make you feel when you sent those souls to damnation?"

I was inconsolable upon hearing her question. "At the time, it felt good, like they got what they deserved."

Mother, escorted by Tiny, moved closer to comfort me. "And now, child?"

"I feel an emptiness, a void that can only be filled with sending more souls to damnation, but there's something else. It just doesn't feel right. Punish, punish, punish. It feels like I'm only here to hurt not nurture. Is 'hurture' a word? It seems that my existence is predicated on accepting the premise that humanity's destiny is damnation, but does my acceptance of this mean it is a fact or I am making it a fact? Is there another way? Am I driving my fate or am I just a passenger along for the ride?"

Feeling my distress, Mother asked a very odd question. "I see you have a special affinity to Our Lady. What brings you to her?"

I looked upwards again at this unblemished lady made in a beautiful white marble and found an easy answer. "She calms me. My mom prayed to her for comfort too, especially at the end."

"Well, what do you think she would tell you right now if she was truly standing in front of you?"

Despondent, I looked away from the statue. "Nothing, I don't deserve her attention."

Mother drew closer and put her hand on my back as well. "Oh, child. You, most of all, deserve her attention. Humanity is consumed by frailty and fears, so much so, that God's children are unable to see the divine spark within them. Every day, the battle between good and evil rages. The beast and the wolf fight for humanity's soul, however, apathy and arrogance sentence the fallen to live in the past, never growing and never learning. The beast seems to be winning. It's time, as the kids say, to grab the wheel and drive. Don't you think?"

The whispering voices returned, calling me to join them. Reverberating repeatedly in my head, they kept a rhythmic beat. "Brother, join us. The wolf waits for you."

"Mother, I hear these voices about the wolf waiting for me. Who are they? Are they good or just more bull....? Ooops, sorry for that." I had to stop myself before swearing in church.

"Child, we are concerned for you. Can you see the world as a wonder and not as something deserving of punishment? We need to nurture more and chastise less. Is the world deserving of punishment or is punishment the world's lifeblood? Do our actions drive the world toward evil? Remember, one action can ripple across time and space, especially for those who like to live in the past. These voices you hear are trying to guide you. Heaven's children need protection."

Listening to Mother's compassion and concern for me failed to provide a sufficient degree of comfort to resolve my ongoing inner battle. The conversation did, however, cause an intense and growing uneasiness within me. "OK, now I have a migraine. Sorry, but I have to go."

Mother removed her hand from my back to allow me to leave. "We'll be with you, wherever you are. Will you come back tomorrow?"

"Sure." Rising to make my exit, I wanted to hug Sister Alicia before leaving. My extended arms were met with her loving embrace. It was a comforting feeling I hadn't experienced for years. As I walked down the aisle to exit the church, I thought about what they had said. Did I want to be a source of pain or relief? Was I worse than the people I judge and punish, unintentionally sowing the seeds of evil and wickedness? I guessed pain is the offspring of pain. The wicked deserve punishment, that was without question; however, did our zeal in dispensing justice take us too far from truth? But a question had been nagging at me for some time. Why were we only dealing with the perpetrators of wickedness on a local level when there were evil doers who operated on a global scale, dwarfing all others? There was a game being played that was not yet readily apparent to me. For now, the beast was winning.

The dock was full of well-wishers, both fake and genuine, that afternoon. Passing through the crowd, I could sense both sadness and relief in the air enveloping me. Apparently, the three miscreants impacted more lives than mine, albeit not as fatally. The crowd's mood validated the action taken and any doubts I may have felt.

At the slip where the boys had normally docked their boat, Kat and Jenny stood holding a wreath. Kat spent a few minutes describing how much the boys were loved. Some eyes rolled in the crowd when she illustrated their wonderful qualities. "The boys were generous and caring individuals who always had time for their friends. Jenny and I will always remember the humor and passion they brought to our everyday lives., whether it was the silly jokes they would tell or the enthusiasm they had for opening the pub. Their energy was boundless and success limitless." With a nod to Jenny, Kat asked her to toss the flowers into the water as a memorial to the boys. Jenny seemed robotic and emotionless as she tossed the flowers into the bay. Who could blame her, considering the years of abuse she took from Decker and the lack of compassion from Kat?

Next, Kat asked the local acapella group to sing a song that would highlight the solemnity of the occasion. The song was old hymn I recalled from attending Mass with my mother, and their rendition was beautiful; however, it would never be the same for me. The song was ruined for all time. These boys didn't deserve to have it sung in their memory.

My dad and Yo-Yo stood off to the side, listening to Kat's eulogy. They didn't seem to mind not being mentioned at any point in Kat's speech. They appeared equally emotionless and taciturn as they watched the spectacle. Perhaps, they finally saw through all the lies.

I continued to survey the crowd, more so to pass the time than anything else. As my attention passed from end of the dock to the other, another piece of my past came into view. Standing at far end of the crowd, physically and spiritually detached from the rank-and-file crowd who were considered below their station, was the Beauty Crew. How good it was to see them.

Immediately recognizable and still fastened to a superficial self-love of their genetic magnificence, they were, in my opinion, a pretentious representation for a gilded generation. There was Chip, the bastion for the suburban elite, who could always demean anyone crossing his path who was not of his social breeding.

Today, he stood silently, head bowed and looking humble. Barclay, Chip's girlfriend, stood next to him, with one hand touching his back and another wiping a tear as her head rested on his shoulder. Bella still radiated an untouchability for 99.999% of the population. Her dark hair, flowing over her shoulders, and olive complexion shimmered in the sunlight. She was accompanied by a man previously unknown to me who seemed like a normal guy. He was someone who would be sitting far away from the BCs at college yet was still an attractive person though not up to their standards. That was puzzling as nothing in her past indicated Bella would be compatible with this sort of fellow, or so I thought. TT was there as well, but she held hands with another girl. I didn't see that one coming. Maybe it was her lack of self-respect or self-confidence that made her date T-Rex or hide in plain sight as they say, but it seems in the years following my death, she found herself. TT was always likable. Now, she seemed like a new person. All of them seemed different to me. They had grown up and matured. I needed to probe the group more deeply.

At the end of the ceremony, Yo-Yo ran over to me, pulling Jenny along with her. I wondered how much she knew of Jenny's ordeal. Yo-Yo always had a profoundly empathic ability for understanding other people's emotions. She understood me as Jo-Jo and me in my current form as Isaac.

Trying to hide her excitement during a solemn event, Yo-

Yo hugged me with one of her nuclear-powered bear hugs. "Hi, Isaac! Thanks for coming. I'm so happy to see you, even though you disappeared for a few days. Hey, you smell yummy again. What's up with that? Are you making cinnamon rolls again?"

Hearing and seeing my sister raised my spirits 100 times in a matter of seconds. "Yo-Yo, you're too funny. It's great to see you. Hi, Jenny, that was a nice ceremony. I'd give you a hug, but someone has a lock tight grip on me."

Yo-Yo didn't hide her disapproval of my comment, "Very funny, big fella. Very funny."

Jenny, still detached from the world, replied somberly, "I'm glad it's over. It was so overwhelming. I just wanted something quiet and small with no theatrics, but that's not Mom's way. She's always got to give it the Broadway treatment."

Yo-Yo still held me in a warm and tight embrace. I wished it could have lasted longer. "I'm sure it's just her way of coping. Yo-Yo, what do you think?"

Jenny was unresponsive and motionless, hands folded and staring wide-eyed toward some far away point. Yo-Yo, on the other hand, was direct in her feelings. "Please, are you kidding me? The stars revolve around Planet Kat. Right sis'?" That comment elicited a smile from Jenny, even bringing a twinkle to her eyes. Yo-Yo, you're a queen. She called her sis'! Was it possible Yo-Yo had been a good and true sister to Jenny these past few years, like she had been with me?

Yo-Yo finally released me from her mega-hug and scanned the crowd for recognizable faces. She quickly noticed my old classmates. "Hey, Jenny, aren't those your friends?"

Jenny was startled for a moment, and quickly broke out of her funk. "Yes, that's the old gang from college. Let's go say hi. Isaac, you come too. I want to introduce you to them."

They held hands as they walked over, and I trailed behind. Looking at them, it was easy to see the girls had bonded over the past three years, and that bond was deeply rooted. Yo-Yo wouldn't do that with just any acquaintance. Watching them together and seeing the connection they shared, sadness had less of a hold over me and no longer engulfed me to the extent it had previously.

A small and uncomfortable smile formed on Jenny's face. "Hi guys, thanks for coming today. You remember Yo-Yo?"

TT was first to offer her condolences. "Of course. Hi, Yo-Yo. We can only imagine how you guys feel right now, losing a brother, husband and good friend, all in one day. We're shaken about T-Rex too. Although he had a lot of growing up to do, he was a unique person."

Her description of T-Rex's life and sympathy for his death struck me oddly. It seemed like a half-hearted attempt at compassion for an old friend. It became apparent that TT was not completely devasted at the loss of T-Rex. I needed to know what had happened over the past three years that brought about this sort of change in a member of the BC.

Others chimed in and asked her how she was doing, while Barclay and Bella held Jenny tightly. Their conversation was punctuated by an uncomfortable silence that normally followed these types of situations. The comfortability of the situation was addressed when Bella asked about me. "Jenny, who's your friend?"

"Oh, how rude of me. This is Isaac Noone. He's been working with JR on his cars and stuff. He's become a good friend of the family too." Jenny then grabbed my left arm softly, unintentionally showing her affection for me.

I waved my hand as a casual greeting and to acknowledge Jenny's introduction. "Hi, it's a pleasure to meet all of you."

One by one, the BCs greeted me, mostly through hand gestures and gentle smiles. All were genuine and sincere. My radar did not pick up any warning signs yet, although I suspected that they noticed Jenny's fondness for me. They looked me over as any normal person would in the current situation.

Feeling it best to leave them, as it would preclude any further possibility for rendering new judgements, I attempted to say farewell. "Well, I should be going. There's a lot to do before I get to sleep tonight."

Bella wouldn't hear it. "No. No. We're about to grab a bite. Why don't you guys come with us? That means you too Yo-Yo. Jenny, it looks like you need to get some food in you. When was the last time you ate?"

Yo-Yo responded for Jenny. "I think that's a great idea. You could use a little distraction right now. I'll go tell Dad and Kat."

Jenny acquiesced, "OK. OK. Let's go." Yo-Yo worked her magic again.

Once Yo-Yo told Dad and Kat of the lunch plan, we were on our way. Jenny and Yo-Yo accompanied me to the restaurant. Luckily for my gastronomic desire, we went to Giuseppe's Kitchen. On the ride, Yo-Yo wanted to play the "I Spy" game. We went through various iterations of sights along the way. It brought smiles to both Jenny and me, further breaking down the walls surrounding Jenny. I think she actually started feeling some semblance of happiness. Every wrong answer she gave prompted a giggle from Yo-Yo. Of course, I added to the pandemonium with each silly guess. I was always terrible at this game. Laughing hard, Yo-Yo made a point of that too. "Geez, Isaac, you are the worst ever at this game. Don't ever go on a game show!"

"Alright, alright, funny girl. That's true." My response was interrupted by Jenny's laughter and radiant glow. It was great to hear and see both again.

We arrived at the restaurant and met the old gang, who were already waiting for us inside. They were whispering to each other as we entered the restaurant, raising my suspicion level. My desire to probe more into their lives was re-energized. I mumbled, "Let the games begin."

Yo-Yo tapped my arm. "What?"

"I said it looks like gang's already here." Whew, that was close.

They waved us over to them. Sitting at the back of the restaurant, they made sure to sit Jenny and me on the bench against the wall. It was obvious they wanted to keep me in a more controllable spot for assessing me and my intentions. The lunch conversation went along amiably and without any red flags being raised. We talked harmlessly and effortlessly about local current events, new clothing styles or what was going to be the next big thing. After a few iced teas, Jenny and Yo-Yo excused themselves to go to the bathroom, providing an opening for some direct interrogation.

Chip was first. "Isaac, you know we are fond of those ladies. We don't want to see either of them hurt. They have been through enough these last few years. What's your angle here? We noticed Jenny's affection for you earlier."

Being careful to respond in a calm manner so as not to illicit concern, I replied softly, "Listen, I know more than you could ever know. The world has taught me many lessons, mostly hard and cruel ones, but my life has been shaped by both good and evil. Jenny and Yo-Yo are pristine souls that are not in danger with me. They are protected. No one, I mean no one, will ever hurt them again."

Chip leaned back in his chair and struck a more contemplative posture. "I hope we can believe you. This all started with Jo-Jo. She hasn't been the same since that day he went missing."

I leaned forward to express my sincerity. "Chip, you can believe me. You may not trust me yet but give me a chance to prove myself."

Everyone at the table became eerily silent. Jenny and Yo-Yo were waiting in line to use the bathroom, which gave us more time to talk.

Barclay chimed in, "This started before Jo-Jo. We all knew something was wrong for some time. Jo-Jo was the tipping point.

God, did Giuseppe start making cinnamon rolls? The odor is driving me crazy."

The group's sincerity hit me as genuine. I appreciated their concern, especially when directed toward Yo-Yo. Chip was about to ask me more about my life being shaped by good and evil; however, he stopped his question mid-sentence as Jenny returned to the table, led by a bouncing Yo-Yo.

TT noticed the difference, "It's good to see you like this. Really good. We've been waiting to see you like this again. Maybe Isaac has something to do with it?"

The direction of the conversation was about to turn a dangerous corner. I needed to divert it before we headed down this unwanted rabbit hole. "Jenny, Yo-Yo, I need to get you home. Thanks for the lunch, everyone. It was great getting to know you better."

TT then asked for a ride. "Do you mind giving Sam and me a lift, since we're going in the same direction?"

"Sure, no problem." It seemed that TT and her friend got the short straw to continue the interrogation, in private this time.

CHAPTER 17

Dropping off Jenny and Yo-Yo at home, I noticed Kat waiting on the porch for us, and she didn't seem very happy. She had a stern yet inquisitive look on her face, cementing my suspicion that she knew Jenny had grown closer to me. It wouldn't be hard to imagine that the three miscreants told her about the connection Jenny and I had made at the coffee shop. She had to know about the cause of Jenny's bruises too. Her manner at the pub opening was a warning sign. A red flag flew at full mast and flapped furiously in a high wind.

Kat walked to the railing and yelled. "JR, the girls are home. Can you stop tinkering with the car for a second? Damn, sometimes I think that car is your wife."

Dad was flustered momentarily. "OK. OK. I hear you. Hey girls. How was lunch?"

Yo-Yo answered cheerfully, which I'm sure Kat didn't like. "It was great, Dad. Wasn't it Jenny?"

"Yup. It was exactly what I needed." Leaning into the car, Jenny thanked us for lunch and said a quick, "See you later guys." Our eyes met and acknowledged our growing feelings for each other.

Yo-Yo went a step further and almost pulled me out of the car window to give me a big kiss on the cheek. As she pulled away, she looked at me with an odd look of confusion. She raised her fingers to her lips and tried to speak but couldn't. I could see my sister's mind working to figure out what just happened. Then in an instant, she opened her eyes wide and clasped her hands together. The expression on Yo-Yo's face could be best described as an *aha moment*.

I looked at her with a sense of dread asked her whether she was feeling alright. Did I accidentally let my guard down and turn on her empathic skills? Did she feel the anguish and torture of the victims that I judged? I opened my mouth to ask another question; however, Yo-Yo raised her index finger to her lips and whispered, "Shhh." She then sprinted up the side staircase like a jackrabbit being chased by a coyote. Watching Yo-Yo scoot into the house, JR and Kat both raised their eyebrows and laughed nervously before saying their goodbyes to me. Dad wondered, "What got into her?" Turning her attention to me, Kat's expression quickly turned to a frown.

I waved at them from the car, looking back at the three of

them standing together, with my dad's arm around Jenny. I could hear Kat telling Jenny, "I don't want you hanging around that boy. Remember, you're a widow now, and I don't trust him."

Stupid pig. She didn't know I could hear her. Smiling and playing it cool still, I asked TT and Sam about their destination. "So, where do you guys live?"

Before driving off, Sam had jumped into the front seat, probably to get a closer look at me. "Not too far, just on the other side of Main. Your name is Isaac Noone, right?"

"Yes, Isaac Michael Noone to be exact."

Sam stared out of the passenger side window, her attempt to show an air of triviality to the conversation. "Great initials. I-M-N. That's I am in, right? Or is it better to say I am no one?"

Her perceived intelligent observation made me laugh. She obviously didn't realize who or what I was. Mockery and razzing Sam were next on the conversation's agenda. I had sensed she had powers while we were at lunch, but I wasn't too worried. The Pale Rider's radar was working perfectly. "I don't know. What do you think witchy poo?"

"You're very perceptive Isaac, if that's your real name. My full name is Samantha Goodefellow. My family was one of the first settlers of Massachusetts, and we survived a shit-storm three hundred years ago, if you know what I mean. My ancestors were hung or burned in the town square for nothing, other than for being different, but that's ancient history. Let's focus on you, shall we? There's something about you that's puzzling me. I could feel power emanating from you at the dock, but I also sensed an internal struggle."

I decided to see how much she knew. Was she a force for good or evil? "Do you want to know who I am? How about you TT, would you like to have the curtains pulled back?"

Her eyes wide open and on the verge of panic, TT responded weakly, "Y-Y-Yes, I would like to know. Sam told me earlier I had nothing to fear, but I'm not so sure now. Everything about you points to fear."

"Well, I'm not that bad." I replied with a smirk, tapping the steering wheel to the beat of mellow tune on the radio.

After driving past a few more streets, TT asked me to park in front of a store that practiced the natural arts. "You can pull in here. This is our store. We live right upstairs. We can have some privacy to finish our conversation if you don't mind. There's so much more to know about you. I can feel it."

"Nice store. Let's go in but aren't you afraid of inviting a stranger into your home? I could be a maniac or a serial killer."

Sam was laser focused on continuing the interrogation and was unfazed on the potential risk I posed. "We're not worried; we can protect ourselves." She was a little overconfident to say the least.

Not knowing where this was going to lead or whether a judgement was going to be rendered, I presented them with one last warning before going into their store. "Last chance ladies. Do you really want to continue our discussion?"

Upon hearing my question, TT became unnerved and took a step back. "What do you mean 'last chance?' Sam, what does he mean? There's something cold and dark about him. It feels like we are walking into a meat grinder."

Grabbing her hands softly, Sam was quick to reassure TT. "Don't worry. He won't be able to hurt us, and for some odd reason, I don't think he will."

Wearing my best *resting dad face* that learned so well from my father, I provided a slightly annoyed response. "Are we going in or not?"

We walked through the store that had been closed for the day. They led me to a back room that was furnished like a normal living room. TT kept her distance from me and turned on a lamp's light at the far end of the room. Sam directed me to the couch and pointed out a spot for me to sit. "Have a seat. Would you like some tea or coffee? Afterall, this is a friendly place."

"Thanks, but no coffee or tea for me. Let's get this party started. You don't have to fear me." I said with a tint of sarcasm, "I won't bite, unless you're wicked and evil, but I don't believe that to be the case. We'll see." I had to throw in a little joke there. "Sorry, just kidding. Now, the best way to describe who I am is to show you. All that I ask is that you hold my hands, and all will be revealed."

With apprehension, they approached and sat next to me, one on each side. The two young witches slowly reached out for my hands. With immediate effect, my true nature revealed itself in a vision of pain and suffering. Sam screamed out with her eyes turning bright white, "Oh heaven save us from Death, the Pale Rider. He is unforgiving vengeance. Why are you here? Why? What are you doing with Jenny's family?"

Both could see my terrible form, staring at them like a ravenous beast stalking its prey. TT stood paralyzed by fear, hearing and seeing Sam's screams, not knowing what to say and unable to break free. The only thing she could move was her bladder. She made a mess of her pants and the couch.

"Oh, I am so much more than that. I am mayhem, havoc, and the judge that comes in the night to render evil souls to hell's fires! Feel and see my pain." At that prompting, TT and Sam saw the day of my death, happy at the start and fatal at the end. One thing that was different this time was the sight of Jenny crying and begging her mom not to do this. We could hear her pleas for forgiveness resonating throughout the vision. "I'm sorry. God, I'm so sorry." It was heartbreaking. Why didn't I remember this earlier? Of course, her mom just slapped her and told her to shut up. Then, I showed them the images of Jenny's rapes. Sobs of heartache and anguish came from both now. They could feel all the pain Jenny suffered from the agony of Decker's molestation as well as my imprisonment in a watery purgatory. They could feel Decker's incestuous hands all over Jenny's body and the extreme violation of his entry into her. His arms were like an octopus, coming out of every direction and impossible for Jenny to control. The vision of Jenny staring blankly, corpse-like, while the repeated violations occurred was a sorrowful sight for all of us. Tears flowed from my eyes.

TT then found her voice, "Oh my God. Jenny, what did they do to you? They're animals, pure evil! How did you survive this misery?" Then turning her attention to me, TT shouted for the whole world to hear, "It's Jo-Jo. I can see him. He's back. I don't understand. Did they kill you? Where were you? So much pain! It's so cold here! So dark!"

Finally, and without hesitation, I admitted what had always been known. "Yes, I'm back. Back from my watery grave to protect the innocent and punish the wicked."

TT wanted to know more. "Was it you that took care of...?"

It was time to end this revelation. "No more questions! Now it's my turn to set things right. Will I have a problem with you?"

Sam was quick to plead, "Please have mercy on us. We won't say anything. We haven't done anything wrong."

"Because if you did, there would be two more souls to stoke hell's fires today, but I don't think I need to worry about it. My vision has made it clear that your souls haven't been tainted by the evil that saturates this world. Stay that way or I'll be back for a visit, and it will be the last one with you on this earth."

With my warning made abundantly clear enough for a blind man to see, I released their hands. They remained stunned and motionless in front of me, never had they considered that my revelation would have reached such heights, or depths for that matter.

Softening my tone, I wanted to put them at ease. "Peace to all of you. Grace surrounds you. Keep it there, or else."

I stood to leave, and TT made one more request. Still shaking from her vision, she struggled to get the words out of her mouth. "Are you here to protect Jenny and Yo-Yo. They mean a lot to us."

With a wink, I replied before departing the store, "Without question. They mean a lot to me too. See you around, ladies. See you around."

CHAPTER 18

I made my way back to Captain's house feeling good about the day. Out front, Tres sat waiting nervously for me to come home. Normally at this time of the day, she would be inside getting belly rubs from Captain after her afternoon walk. She hated being alone too. Something was up.

"Hey, how's my big girl? Who's a happy girl? Yes, you are, aren't you?" She quickly snapped out of her little funk as she tried to jump into my arms. I opened the door to the house, and Tres backed away whimpering. She would not follow. Sensing an ominous turn of events for me, I paused for a moment to prepare myself for whatever danger could be inside.

Opening the door slowly and gazing deeply into the interior of the house, my danger-sensing radar began to overheat. Who or what was in there? I could see Captain talking to someone in the kitchen who was out of my line of sight. The visitor's sinister tone was eerily familiar. Captain's tone was completely opposite, more deferential than defiant as he tried to provide an explanation to some problem that the visitor did not want to entertain. Cutting off his every sentence, the visitor's voice grew exponentially more sinister.

"Listen Buddy Boy, you need to get him with the program! No more handling him with kid gloves. We need to pick up the pace. I have high, sorry, I mean low hopes for the new member of our family. Hey, Jo-Jo, I know you're there. Get your ass in here."

It was like a flash of lightening hit me when I recognized the voice. He was the voice in the abyss, the one about whom the other whisperers warned me. "I'm here. What's the problem?"

The man I saw in the kitchen looked like any other person, inconspicuous and unassuming. He looked like a shopper at the local mall who had a wife, minivan, and 2.2 kids. His only remarkable features were those piercing eyes, that were cold and black.

Annoyed at the lecturing, Captain grumbled and introduced his guest to me. "Jo-Jo, this is Uncle Trick, the boss. He wants you to get work done faster. No more games."

Opening the fridge to grab a cold drink, I answered with youthful arrogance. "He's not my boss, and justice was served recently if you recall." Damn, the fridge was still full of eggs.

Uncle Trick moaned at my response and smug attitude. "You little shit! Who do you think you are? I have seen so many arrogant monkeys like you over countless millennia. That's what I think of humanity, your people. Do you understand our state of affairs?"

Captain jumped right in, "Yes, he does. He's young and still learning. He still has the mind of a teenager, but his potential is limitless."

At that suggestion, Uncle Trick smiled and raised his arms to me. "Listen, no one could ever say I'm not fair, but my patience is wearing thin. There's a job to do and it won't get done on its own. Straighten up and fly right Buddy Boy. We're counting on you."

He walked toward me slowly and deliberately until he stood face to face with me. I took note of the rancid odor emanating from his mouth. It smelled like a mixture of rotten garbage blended with diarrhea and baby diapers. From that cesspool of a mouth came an ominous threat. "Well Jo-Jo, the pain your three friends felt will pale in comparison to what I'll do to you two misguided fools. I expect results, boys." The expression on this face became cold and intimidating to accentuate the threat to us. "Did you really think humanity was capable of being saved, or even redeemed. Hell, no. I look at you and see someone who squandered his chance at life. No redemption for you is coming.

All that can be done, or needs to be done, is to send people to me faster. Hell's fires demand more. Do you want to be at the top or the bottom of the food chain? Think about that for a while." His evil laughter filled the room. Then Uncle Trick did something creepy even for him. He put his nose next to my jawline and took in a big breath. "Mmm, the power is intoxicating. I haven't smelled something like that for hundreds of years. I knew from the start you were going to be special. How special remains to be seen."

His reaction sickened me. It did, however, make me think of mom and Yo-Yo. They knew something about me and so did Uncle Trick. My response was loaded with sarcasm. "Back off Buddy Boy. And you could really use a breath mint too."

Uncle Trick, slightly amused by my comments, tilted his back and laughed mockingly. "This kid's a pistol, a real pistol but you'll learn your place." Our unwelcomed guest turned to leave and whistled a menacing tune. "OK boys. Bye for now. I'll be seeing you soon. Don't disappoint me, boys." Out the door and into oblivion he went, continuing his evil laugh. I knew he was gone once Tres ran back into the house.

I rushed toward Captain and slammed my hands on the kitchen table. "This is insane. What are we doing? We can't give into him."

Captain rubbed his head with vigor, understanding the

meaning Uncle Trick's visit and threats. "Enough for today. I have a headache. Why don't you take Tres out and see your girlfriend?"

That was a great idea. I wanted to see Jenny again and to feel her close to me. I needed reassurance, a reminder on who I was, before this journey entered its final act.

CHAPTER 19

"Tres, let's go for a ride. Maybe we'll see Jenny." Tres was wagging her tail uncontrollably; the word *ride* always had that effect on her. Getting into the car, I saw the wolf had returned to visit me. It sat regally across the street at the edge of the woods staring at the two of us. Tres stared back and tilted her head, first at the wolf and then at me. The whispering voices started again, bidding me to act, "Jo-Jo, reject the beast, accept the wolf. Heaven waits for you." Their voices echoed in my mind as I stood watching that noble animal. The wolf ended the visit with a howl that resonated throughout the neighborhood and appeared to be calling me forward. In the blink of an eye, it ran into the woods, leaving me to contemplate my future. The battle was getting clearer by the minute, but I needed to see Jenny.

Pulling out of the driveway, I called Jenny to see if she was keen for a meeting or perhaps a little late afternoon delight. Jenny answered my call quickly. We chatted for several minutes about how she was doing before I asked about a rendezvous at the Fisherlady again. At first, she was unsure about meeting me, but ultimately felt the desire to talk to someone she could trust. "I just need to talk to someone who wants nothing from me and who won't judge me. I can't put this burden on Yo-Yo, especially not with the things I've seen."

I assumed the person she trusted was me. Of all the people she knew and of all the friends she had, was I correct in believing that Jenny wanted to be with me when she unwrapped her heart? Still, I proceeded with caution. We made plans to meet at the boat in about half an hour. The tone of her voice was different, which was understandable, considering the events of the day; however, the conversation didn't sit well with me.

I drove toward the dock, thinking about all the great qualities Jenny had. The day of betrayal was far in the rear-view mirror now. Being with her and trying to ease her pain occupied my every thought. As I neared the parking lot, my brain told me to get over to Jenny's house right away. Something was wrong. I immediately burned rubber out of the parking lot and rushed to Jenny's house. Terrible thoughts rang through my mind. Dear God, please don't let me be late.

I pulled into the driveway and noticed that Jenny's car was still there. No one else appeared to be home. Ringing the doorbell repeatedly and banging on the front door with ferocity did not receive a response. At that point, one of the neighbors heard the commotion and asked what was wrong.

"I think Jenny is in trouble. Something's wrong. We need to get in quickly. Do you have a key?"

The neighbor turned to run back home. "At my house, wait a minute."

"There's no time." I immediately pushed open the door with the strength of one kick to the lock. We both ran in, calling for Jenny repeatedly while we searched the first-floor rooms. We met at the base of the stairs that led the second floor and immediately heard the sound of running water from upstairs. We sprinted up the stairway to the bathroom where horror met us. We found Jenny motionless in the bathtub with her wrists cut, tears flowing from her eyes and her precious blood filling the tub. From her pale skin color and the amount of blood flowing out, she was at death's door.

I yelled to the neighbor to call 911 and pulled Jenny out of the tub. I grabbed some towels to cover her sliced wrists and held them tightly until the paramedics came. The minutes past like hours until they could arrive and relieve me. For those precious few minutes, I yelled at Jenny to stay awake and to not give up. I told her how special she was. "Jenny, don't you realize how wonderful you are! Please hold on! You can't leave me. Mother of God, please help her! I beg you! Mother, please!"

"Isaac, please let me go. You don't understand what I've done, what my family has done. It's not right. Please let me go.

I'm not worth it." Her voice was shaky and tearful.

I refused to give up on her. Holding her wounds tightly, I pulled her further out of the tub and embraced her tenderly. "Jenny, you are worth it. None of it is your fault. I know, Slim. I know everything."

As soon as she heard being called Slim again, Jenny began to cry. "How do you know that name?"

"Jenny, see me as I truly am." Transforming into Jo-Jo, a bright light filled the room. I needed Jenny to see me in my true form, but she was weak from the loss of blood. She tried with all of her remaining strength to focus on me.

Struggling mightily, she gathered enough strength to open her eyes and to see a sight from her past. "Jo-Jo, you're alive? How can this be?"

"Alive? I'm something different, indescribably different. But I want you to understand that I know everything. Everything! You need to live and love yourself, because I do." It was then, like a lightning bolt, that I finally understood my mother's advice to me all those years ago. Mom always said, "Love yourself, please."

Jenny could only look at me and cry. The sadness in her eyes was heartbreaking. "I'm so sorry. I should have been stronger. Why didn't I warn you?" Her voice and body were still weak, but her eyes still had a special sparkle.

I rested my cheek to her head. "There was nothing you could have done. Now, stay with me. The paramedics are here."

Just as the paramedics were arriving, Dad, Yo-Yo, and Kat came home. They ran into the house panicking. Their neighbor had called to inform them of what Jenny had tried to do and what I had done to save her. One of the EMTs asked Kat to stay downstairs, even though she demanded to go up, while they stabilized Jenny. I continued to hold onto her sliced wrists and still prayed to the Virgin to intercede. We had to synchronize the removal of my hands of her wounded wrists to ensure more blood wouldn't be lost. I moved my hand off one arm then the other as soon as the EMTs were ready. After a few minutes of intense work, they stabilized Jenny and brought her down on a stretcher as I trailed behind. Jenny was quickly loaded into the ambulance and rushed to the local hospital.

Rushing to the car, Dad and Yo-Yo thanked me for saving Jenny as they wanted to get to the hospital quickly. Kat, on the other hand, believed I was at fault to some degree. "I know you had something to do with this. You got a little too close while she was married. Now she's a widow. You played around with her and didn't care about her mental state."

Dad tried to calm her down, "Kat, I don't think Isaac did any of that. He just saved Jenny. Let's get to the car quickly. We need to go to the hospital." Fumbling with his keys, he asked their next-door neighbor to stay with Yo-Yo until they returned, as the hospital was not a place for her.

Kat continued to look at me wild eyed and with a fatal intent. I walked to the car with them, staying silent for the most part. As I held the door open for Kat, I gave her a nice send-off with a whisper that only she could hear, "Well, Mannion, I'll be seeing you."

Staring wide-eyed at me, Kat's reaction was a perfect shock to her system.

Not hearing me, dad asked Kat what I had said. An uneasy Kat replied, "Oh, nothing. Just said see you later."

As they backed out of the driveway, Kat, terrified and shaken, was fixated on Tres and me. The endgame was nearing its conclusion.

CHAPTER 20

I had a sleepless night, not because I was worried about Jenny, rather due to the exhilaration of potentially being at the end of my journey. Jenny was going to make it; I could feel it in my bones. Tossing and turning all night, Tres was there watching over me to her amusement. Every time I rolled over to the side of the room where she slept, she was there, perfectly positioned to give me one of her monster-sized licks. "Thank you very much, but please stop," was my answer all night. Of course, Tres wouldn't listen to that command.

The next morning, Captain and I decided to take the Fisherlady out early. After the meeting with Uncle Trick, Captain needed to feel the wind and to savor the aroma of the open seas as a way of re-centering himself. He was a complete grouch for the entire ride to the boat, complaining about everything under the sun. I asked him, "We're going to need a chainsaw to cut that huge hair across your ass today, aren't we?"

After mumbling something in Portuguese, he started to

laugh. "We may need something stronger." For the rest of ride, we were consumed with laughter.

Arriving at the boat well before the other crews did, we immediately started loading our gear as Captain didn't want to delay shoving off. While Captain and I were stocking the inside cabin, we heard a commotion on the dock. Kat had driven to the dock and was angrier than a hornet. Dad and Yo-Yo were there as well trying to reason with her. Dad was blocking her in a futile attempt to stop her from getting on the boat. "Kat, stop. This is crazy."

"Leave me alone. He knows something about the boys. He's been playing us, all this time. He's a fraud."

Captain and I watched the action play out, bemusedly waiting for Kat's next move. Ultimately, after several more minutes of pushing and arguing, Kat was able to move my father out of the way and jumped onto the boat, holding a revolver. "Isaac, I know you're responsible for everything that's happened to my family. Admit it. Admit it."

Tres was ready to pounce on Kat, but Captain ordered her to heel. He didn't want to see his baby get hurt.

"Your family? That's beautiful." I stood in front of her, laughing and unshaken by Dad's bewilderment. "Listen, the time has come to end the misery you and your family have caused. JR and Yo-Yo are not your family. They belong to another whom you murdered, a murdered son of a murdered mother. Should we talk about them, Mannion?"

Kat was quick to scream a reply, "No. No. No. You're a liar!"

Dad looked like he was hit by a ton of bricks. Motionless and his mouth opened wide, he could barely speak. His lips moved but no words could be formed at first. Summoning up the strength to speak, he turned his attention Kat and asked weepily, "Kat, what is Isaac talking about? Is, is your name Mannion?"

Still in shock at the revelation, Kat tried to give a coherent response. She shouted, "JR, don't listen to him. I'm a good person. I'm a good person." It's always humorous when someone gets caught with their hands in the proverbial cookie jar, they don't seem to answer the question asked.

It was my turn to respond. "Silence, whore. You asked for chaos, and it has come for you." I was in the process of changing to my terrifying form when I caught sight of Yo-Yo crying. I couldn't do it. Not in front of her, never. Instead of Death, I appeared in front of them as Jonah.

"Yo-Yo jumped onto the deck and hugged me. She cried out, "I prayed for you to come back to us. I prayed every day."

Dad was in shock, with tears flowing from his eyes. "Jonah, is that you? Is that really you? My son?"

Seeing my dad's face and holding Yo-Yo tightly, my voice trembled. "Dad. Yes, it is, sort of."

"I don't understand, where were you? Who is Isaac? What is going on?"

"Jonah was murdered like his mom by Kat Mannion to satisfy a misplaced grudge from a long time ago." I pointed to Kat and emphasized my point. "Now I am something different. I have come back to judge the wicked, the purveyors of evil who have inflicted pain, suffering and misery to our family. Kat, let's talk about how much money you've stolen from my dad, as you promised me to do three years ago. Or should we talk about Jenny too? Let's talk about how you knew Decker frequently violated Jenny and did nothing about it except to blame her."

Kat shook her head in disbelief at my revelation. "No, what are you saying? How could you have known?"

With that, I leaped across the deck and took hold of Kat's arm and showed her all her recent sins. While the others were frozen in time, motionless on the deck, Kat went through the cycle of the pain she caused. Her screams of pain and suffering rang loud, escalating to an almost operatic level. She saw the repeated rapes of her daughter, and the evil acts that both Decker and Riley

210

committed over the years. Kat could feel the pain of people who were treated as animals and animals treated as dirt. She relived her embezzlement activities and Yo-Yo's smothering confinement during the last few years, even though my dad treated her only with kindness. The icing on the cake was seeing the sisterly bond Jenny and Yo-Yo formed. They shared a purity of love that only sisters could have. The endless nights of giggling and recounting the daily events struck at the very core of her heart.

"No, I'm not a bad person. I'm not a bad person." She fell to the floor crying and detached from reality. Suddenly grasping the reality and totality of her errors, Kat became subdued, "My life is ruined. My family is ruined."

I decided the time had come to end this revelation and released Kat from my grip. Backing away from her, I instantaneously turned into the Pale Rider to the horror of my family. I had to, even if Yo-Yo saw. Kat's entire revelation pushed me on that path. At first, they were paralyzed with fear at my terrifying appearance, but as I approached Kat, keen on dispensing justice, Yo-Yo grabbed hold of me tightly again. She pleaded with me, "Please don't do it. She's not worth it. Killing her won't give you peace. It won't even give any of us peace. You'll just lose another part of your soul. I see you! Mom sees you!"

As I looked at my sister and the pitiful sight of Kat

mumbling to herself on the deck, my heart began to soften. It was sufficiently odd that Mom's teachings resonated again with me. I recalled one of her last lessons to me. He gentle voice reverberated in my mind. "We can't allow history to imprison us to a predictable future. We need to make history and not have history make us. Living in the past allows for mistakes to repeat and grow ever more serious as we find better ways to hurt each other, faster and more often. We remember the trauma in our lives and never let it go. We keep it with us, rooted so deeply that it guides our action or inaction to a fait accompli. Growth stops, other than allowing our pain to fester and flourish. Pain can be real or perceived, but its cause is never explored and truly remedied. Instead, our focus is on the pain itself. The past cannot be an absolute truth. Too often, we take the path of least resistance by allowing the past to consume us, missing its lessons that should open our minds and hearts toward a brighter future. We need to meet our pain head-on and then reject it. We need to focus on creating an environment where people can remain in grace and not solely focused on punishing those who injured us. If we expect people to fail, they will. Humanity needs to face the sun and bask in its glow and not continually worry solely about the darkness left by a setting sun. The sun rises again, it always does."

Mom finished that last lecture with a quote written two thousand years ago by the Roman philosopher, Livy. It was a perfect assessment for me that day. "The sun has not yet set for all time." Mom was an encyclopedia of great quotes.

"Kat, this is your one chance to save your life and everlasting soul. Repent and atone for the life you have led. If you don't, you'll have another visit from me, one that will be fatal and fiery at its conclusion."

All Kat could do was to mumble uncontrollably, "I'm so sorry. JR, I'm so sorry. My family. My family."

Returning to my Isaac form, I could only watch the pitiful sight that had once been the object of my fear and hatred. Dad and Yo-Yo could only watch as well.

Captain sat to the side shaking his head, obviously unhappy with the finality of the event. "Uncle Trick is not going to be pleased with us. I hope you're happy now."

"Captain, I'm not sure what to say. You know my mother was a history teacher. She loved to tell stories about people, both good and bad."

Captain rubbed his forehead in exasperation to demonstrate the pain he felt about a potential forthcoming lecture. "Oh my God, not another one of your lessons. You're giving me a migraine."

"Aww c'mon. Please hear me out. Just one quick quote. Do you know Cicero, a man before his time? Over 2,000 years ago, this influential Roman philosopher once said, 'Any man can make mistakes, but only a fool persists in error.' Maybe it's time to end this persistent and foolish behavior, not just for the people we judge but for us too? Well, I think that's what my mom would say if she were here right now."

Turning to my dad, I had difficulty finding the right words, but he didn't have that problem. "Jo-Jo, is that really you? What does this all mean?" He sobbed and hugged me like he never had before, showing me that he really did love me. "I've missed you every minute for the past three years. I wasn't the father you needed or deserved."

"Dad, you did nothing wrong. You could never have prepared me for what happened. No one could have, but you'd better call the police. Attempted murder is attempted murder after all. No more tears, Dad. This is where I'm supposed to be, and Yo-Yo and Jenny need you." After hugging me for a few more seconds, he backed away slowly, shaking his head in silent agreement, and made the call to the police.

As soon as I finished speaking, the howling of a wolf echoed across the dock to everyone's amazement. Visible only to me but audible to all, the magnificent animal continued to howl for nearly a minute; he approved of what I had done.

The other arriving crews gathered on the dock to see what was happening. "Do you hear a howl? Isn't she the lady we saw here yesterday, whose family died in the boat fire recently? Someone said she tried to kill Isaac. Did you see what happened?" Murmuring from the newly formed crowd continued unabated as more spectators came to the dock.

The police soon came and took Kat away after taking the requisite information from all the parties there. The lead detective agreed that Kat's mental state was concerning as she continued her ramblings. They agreed that taking her to the nearby state psychiatric facility for observation and custody was the best plan at this time. My dad agreed to go with the officers to get Kat situated.

By this time, TT and Sam arrived at the dock. I could overhear Sam whispering to TT that she had a premonition of Kat acting erratically at the docks this morning. She had a similar one yesterday but apparently was too afraid to go to Jenny's house, as she had feared that Jenny was being judged and executed by me. Her visions were often confusing or incomplete, apparently. She realized that her fears were unjustified when Yo-Yo called them last night to disclose Jenny's attempted suicide and my actions to save her. I'm not sure how Sam's powers worked but things seemed clearer to her now.

Dad asked for their help, "TT, do you mind staying with Yo-Yo? I need to go with Kat."

"No question, Mr. Evermore. We'll stay with her for as

long as you need us."

"Thanks, I don't want her to be alone."

Looking back at me, before climbing into the waiting ambulance, Dad expressed his gratitude, "Thank you. Thank you for everything you've done." I smiled back, tapping my heart to show him how I felt.

Dad did ask a couple questions before departing. "Is that the boat's captain who's been watching us? How is he part of all this?"

I smiled in response. "Don't worry about him. He's good." Looking at Yo-Yo, I knew she could use another companion. With Tres, I knew Yo-Yo would in good hands, or paws. It would be good to keep Tres away from the forthcoming confrontation with Uncle Trick as well. "Tres, go with Yo-Yo. Keep her safe, big girl." Tres didn't have to be told twice. She ran right over to Yo-Yo, giving her a volume of kisses, too numerous to count.

TT and Sam were both amused by Tres' affection for Yo-Yo. Tres provided them a sloppy greeting to their delight too. They waved to me before leaving.

We would later find out that after a few days of medical observation, Kat was committed to a psychiatric facility.

Ultimately, there would be no trial, and no need for me to testify. She rambled continuously about all the pain she had caused by her misdeeds and that Death was coming to take her away. Her punishment was just and enduring. I thought about sending her an engraved drool cup that said "Mannions Never Lose". Well, not really, I wasn't that cruel, but I could be.

As the last spectators left the dock, Captain and I were left alone on the Fisherlady to contemplate our next meeting with Uncle Trick. We knew it wasn't going to be good, and we needed to be ready.

"Jo-Jo, you continue to amaze me. I don't know how, but you did a good thing today. Now, hell's coming for us, and they won't make us wait long."

"Giddy-up."

CHAPTER 21

Captain and I decided it was best to go home and await the inevitable battle between good and evil. On the drive back to the house, I posed the question to Captain whether we were essentially good by nature, or perhaps we were merely less evil than those forces about to battle us. Was that the best we could hope for, or could we endeavor to something higher, to be something of greater value?

I had focused my entire new existence on fighting against the Seven Deadly Sins instead of nurturing the Seven Heavenly Virtues. It was a concept of *hurturing* not nurturing that drove me. We accidently cultivated sins when we pretended to aspire to heaven. Did heaven want us to solely punish the wicked for what we believe is right? What was driving us? Ignorance, born of sloth, would lead to more pain and suffering. Never to be confused with stupidity, ignorance was a self- inflicted wound. Sloth, fastened with its primary offspring ignorance, was the worst and the most indescribable sin of all, as it incubated the others, especially pride. These frailties drove humanity onto the wrong path, deeper and deeper into the abyss with each passing transgression. In the end, these fatal flaws led to one thing, tears. Tears propagated cruelty which in turn propagated more tears, a never-ending cycle.

"Jo-Jo, I don't know what's right or wrong, up or down, or whatever anymore. Do you remember my story? My journey started on the open seas fully embracing the Seven Deadly Sins, living a life of lust, greed, gluttony and pride. There wasn't much I didn't do. You could probably name it and I did it, with gluttonous passion. Then, like a bolt of lightning, an angel fell from heaven and into my life. Aanshi was truly a gift from heaven. It is still difficult to imagine that a princess could love me. Me? After her death, wrath became my companion and I never looked back. Now, I just don't know anymore."

Captain was motionless behind the wheel of his truck, pondering the existence he had led for these past five centuries. All that moved were his lips, mumbling about the sadness of his current state through successive murmuring cadences of fool, gullible, and horrible. It became evident that he was hitting bottom, emotionally and spiritually, his future resting precariously on a knife's edge. Soon, we would know our fate.

Driving home, a strange mist formed over the town. Oddly though, this mist emanated from the center of town outwards and not from the sea. Pulling into the driveway, the source of the mist became abundantly clear to us. It was coming from Captain's house. With a slight giggle, Captain interjected some levity to our current grave situation. "What did you say earlier? Giddy-up?"

I laughed for a moment with him, further invigorated. Then with a more serious tone, he asked, "Are you ready for what's to come? He won't be alone, and heaven won't help us."

Determined and focused on controlling my own destiny, I stared out the passenger widow toward the house. I replied firmly, "I'm ready, though I think you're wrong. God, and heaven, have always been with us. We just didn't want to acknowledge it. I am beginning to understand what my mom was trying to tell me for so long. We find God, his spirit or whatever you want to call it, in ourselves, waiting for acceptance. If we can learn to love ourselves, we will feel heaven's companionship, no matter what may come. I just hope I'm strong enough. It sounds silly, but we need to fight for what's right and not purely for punishment's sake. Heaven is not angry, it is crying. God is not a warrior seeking to punish. Rather, He is an enduring part of us, stubbornly ingrained in our spirit."

Captain listened patiently, nodding his head as I finished my speech. "OK, Jo-Jo, let's go." We walked slowly to the front door, warily looking around us. We could feel dark presences, but didn't know where and how many there were?

"Gentlemen, please come in." Uncle Trick's sinister voice

echoed through the house and into the front yard. "You've been naughty boys." His seemingly harmless message hid an ominous meaning that failed to intimidate us, well partly anyway.

We walked into the house, prepared for battle. Uncle Trick sat on the La-Z-Boy in the corner of the main room, flanked by four demons on each side. In one hand, he held a cane which he tapped repeatedly in an attempt to distract us. With the other hand, his fingers slowly and repetitively scratched at the arm of the leathery chair, adding to our apprehensive mood. "Well, Buddy Boys, what am I going to do with you? After all the good things I've done for you guys, you go ahead and disappoint me. And Jo-Jo, didn't you think I would find out you were hanging around that damn church."

The volume of his voice rose, emphasizing the gravity of the situation we were in. "You must think free will applies to you as well. It doesn't! You belong to me! Your existence belongs to me! Your souls belong to me!"

He paused momentarily before rising from his perch, walking toward us and softening his tone. "Listen, I'm not unreasonable. Let's look past this little indiscretion and get back to work." He laid his hands on our shoulders to emphasize the power he had over us.

I found the courage to growl a response, "Go to hell and take your friends with you. Our souls can't be taken or given.

They belong to heaven. Don't you find it odd, we never go after the big fish, the ones who are the large-scale perpetrators of evil? These miscreants are allowed to live for years to perpetuate greater evil, but not the ones we deal with. Isn't that you're real plan? Keep the industry of pain and evil alive but feed hell its token few, knowing that this also helps your plan? It's a good business for you."

Uncle Trick didn't like what I had to say. The truth can be a difficult pill to swallow. All these years of deception and the answer was always there in front of us, hanging like a giant pinata being thrashed insatiably by humanity as the only way to get at its contents. Instead of just having a little faith in ourselves and others, we could have seen past the deception and the lies.

Uncle Trick and friends growled. One particularly ugly demon barked, "I told you he was trouble from the start." Uncle Trick showed his unhappiness by punching me hard in the chest, sending me across the room and denting the far wall. Captain tried to intervene but one of the Trick's demons knocked him over before he could help.

Captain and I rose to our feet and joined the battle with ferocity. We fought valiantly from room to room, but the problem is you can't kill something that's not technically alive. Put one down and it gets back up. I continued to lash out, "You will never have us again." Changing into our ghastly form, we battled hard.

We were bloodied but not beaten. The demons fought hard as well and were unyielding.

Finally, they were able to subdue us, holding us down by their sheer numbers. At the point of extreme exhaustion, we changed back to our human form. Uncle Trick decided to employ his psychological warfare on us.

"So, Buddy Boys, where is your God now? He doesn't care about you. He is indifferent to your plight, a father that has abandoned his family when the world was young and never looked back. What a joke! Now do you understand? You're honoring a deadbeat!"

"Captain, we can't listen to him. We need to stand firm." I pleaded with him, but we both began to falter. His brainwashing began to crawl into our brains as the words *deadbeat* and *absentee father* echoed throughout the room. I tried to fight but he was too strong. Then, I heard it, the howl of a wolf, shaking the both of us back to our senses.

I screamed out, "God. Mother. Please help us." An eerie silence encapsulated the room, before an odd sound came from above us and outside the house. We all, including Uncle Trick, looked up, attempting to understand what was coming. Captain, equally puzzled as I was, asked, "Is that the sound of wings?"

The sound came closer to us as we lay prone on the floor

under the demons' grip. Standing over us and still looking upward, Uncle Trick responded with note of a sad resignation, "Damn. It's him. Why did he have to come?" Captain and I would soon discover the identity of this mystery guest. The room was eerily silent again.

Kicking in the front door, Tiny marched into the room with authority. "Greetings, brother, have you missed me?" Tiny punched Uncle Trick savagely, sending him reeling across the room.

The others whispered and released us from their grasp, "It's Michael, the warrior. The warrior is here."

Other spirits appeared out of the vapor. These weren't normal spirits, rather they were my ancestors, Native American warriors summoning the spirit of the wolf from within me. Captain saw his ancestors as well, including his beloved Aanshi holding their children. These ghostly specters put their hands on our shoulders to reinforce our courage and will, whispering to us, "Be strong. You're not alone. Don't believe the Great Deceiver's lies."

Captain was fixated on Aanshi and his children. Tears flowing from his eyes and trembling, he cried out to her, "Aanshi, forgive me. I couldn't save you. Why couldn't I have saved you?"

Aanshi was quick to reply, "Joao, my beloved. Please look

inward and find yourself again, see us as we once were. The more you punish the world the more you punish yourself. It's time to heal."

Captain continued sobbing at the sight of his family. "I miss you so much. I don't know who I am anymore."

"You are loved by us and all those that have come before. Now love yourself and you'll be unconquerable." Turning her attention away from Captain, Aanshi spoke directly to me, "Jo-Jo, thank you for bringing my beloved back to us. The Great Deceiver can't win if you won't let him have power over you." Pausing a moment, Aanshi continued, "Jo-Jo, there's someone who wants to see you."

Out of the vapor, Sister Alicia came walking towards me, but slowly changing into the visage of my mom. I couldn't contain my emotions as I too cried and trembled, "Mom, is that you? I don't understand."

"I've been with you all along, trying to help you with the aid of my heavenly friends. I didn't want to fail you again, but we needed you to see the truth and choose your destiny. And you have, my son. You have." Mom gently pressed her hands on my heart, before telling me how proud she was of me. "You have never disappointed me. I wish you would stop feeling disappointed in yourself. You were always your own worst critic."

Uncle Trick panicked, his voice trembling, "Silence, all of you." Tiny, or should I say Michael, sent him reeling across the room again. "Enough! Back to your wretched abyss, brother."

One of the demons tried to sneak up behind Michael, but to no avail. Michael saw him easily. He grabbed him by the throat and held him like a rag doll. "And what do you think you're doing?" He knocked him through the wall and into the kitchen.

The demons continued their battle with us; however, this time it would be different. We were fortified by the spirits of our ancestors, our history. Each attempt on us was easily turned away. The demons were sent reeling across the room, breaking furniture with each punch.

Uncle Trick finally admitted defeat. Exasperated and full of rage, he hissed his concession. "Fine, you win today, but remember, I will always be around. The best thing about free will is humanity's inability to see the price they pay for it." Turning to the demons, he ordered them back to hell, "Back, back. Down with you, wretches." With that, they wailed in defeated and backed away. Slowly dematerializing into the ether, the demons taunted us with one last evil threat and laugh. "Bye for now boys. See you soon."

I returned my focus to my mother, crying tears of joy. Being able to see her again was all that mattered now. It was amazing that her warmth could still be felt in death.

"Please tell your father and Chiara, I will always love them and that I'll be watching. We must go now. We all love you. Jo-Jo, you know what it takes to be a warrior, be the one who humanity needs."

Both Captain and I pleaded for them to stay, but we knew they had return to heaven. Our job on earth wasn't finished yet. Captain and I returned the sofa back to its normal upright position to rest our weary bones amongst the carnage of broken furniture. Michael, hands on hips and flashing his superhero pose stayed with us.

"Jo-Jo, thank you for saving my soul. I still don't know how you did it." Captain said with a laugh abbreviated by the pain of several bruised ribs and a sore jaw. Looking around the room, he shook his head. "This place is a mess. I don't think my house cleaning service is going to like me. I could use a beer."

I agreed with him wholeheartedly. "Me too, my friend. Me too."

We rose from the sofa and staggered to the kitchen for our reward. Michael stopped us and put his hands on our shoulders. "Nice work, gentlemen. We are all proud of you. I didn't think you could do it. I was wrong. Well, there's a first time for everyone." He smiled at his last comment; however, we didn't share his dry humor.

Captain and I thanked him, but still wished for a couple of beers.

Michael informed us he was leaving and walked to the front door. Turning back to us, he had one last thing to say to Captain. "Considering all that you've experienced, do you still believe your gifts come from the abyss? They are from heaven's grace, but it was easy for my fallen brother's lies to distort your mind. Losing faith in humanity is the trap. Keeping faith in them will sustain you. You are their protectors and nurturers, not punishers. Look to heaven and to maintain the bonds of the Trinity. You still have a job to do. There will be losses but many more victories. Do you understand now?"

We looked at each with a slightly puzzled look. I responded first with a painful grunt. "I think so. What about you Captain? Do you feel enlightened."

Captain responded like the comedian that he always was. "Sure. Like a 100-watt lightbulb."

Michael smiled. "Well, that's all we can expect for now. Got to fly now. See you around. Rest assured, I will." Michael spread his wings and darted to the sky. The image of his winged flight was magnificent and graceful. We took a moment to stare at the beauty of Michael's journey through the air, until this brief peace was humorously broken.

Captain grumbled, "He could have grabbed us a couple of beers before he left, you know." Our laughter was met with painfully sore ribs. For some reason unknown to me, our earthly bodies could feel pain. We'd have to get our own beers.

CHAPTER 22

After a few days, I decided to go to the hospital to check on Jenny, figuring it was best to leave her to the care of professionals. Arriving at the hospital early in the afternoon, I walked in hoping they would allow me to see her. The staff at the front desk advised me that they were only allowing immediate family members to visit patients. It was upsetting to say the least as I did want to see Jenny again. I was still grieving for her.

Turning to leave, I saw Mother Superior and Tiny walking up to the desk. I still called him Tiny but not to his face. There's no doubt that would result in bodily pain for me. Mother spoke to the nurse first, "Good afternoon, dear. I think we can let this fine young man visit. He is a very close friend of the family. Don't worry, we'll walk him in."

"Well then of course, Mother Superior, you don't have to tell me twice."

After getting my pass to enter, the three of us walked to

Jenny's room. "Mother, thank you for this. It's good to have friends in high places."

Mother smiled. Even Tiny, I mean Michael, had what appeared to be a smile forming on his otherwise granite face.

"So, you work here too?"

"Child, I work everywhere."

We continued down the hall to a waiting elevator. On the ride up, I wanted to ask Mother so many questions but was afraid to ask. Who was she? What was her part in this grand play? The words just wouldn't come out of my mouth.

"Tongue tied?" Mother asked gently.

"Was that really a question?" My response was tinted with both humor and sarcasm, knowing she would never take offense. I tried to ask the real question on my mind, but it was proving to be a difficult task. After a few more steps, the words came to me, well partially anyway. "Mother, are you….?"

"Child, I'm here for you. That's who I am."

As we approached Jenny's room, Mother placed her hand on my arm stopping me before parting, "Well, this is as far I should go today. Jo-Jo, can I call you Jo-Jo?"

"Yes, I would never disagree with you, again that is."

Smiling, Mother looked at me with the sort of gentle gaze that only a mother could give. "Well, Jo-Jo, the first part of your journey is nearly finished. What will you do with Jenny now? She needs to heal, but with the love of a good family she can still have a wonderful life."

I paused while I contemplated my sensible response. "Yes, she can, but not with me."

"No child, not with you."

"Jenny has a good father and sister now. I know that she'll be ok. Can I ask you to help her? Maybe have Tiny, I mean Michael, check on them from time to time."

"We will both be around. You know what? We'll go in with you to say a quick hello to everyone too. Shall we?" Mother placed her hand in my arm and escorted me into Jenny's room. Dad and Yo-Yo were in there already, each holding Jenny's hand. Part of the sparkle that had been in Jenny's eyes had started to re-emerge. Seeing me raised the sparkle level up a couple notches.

Mother greeted everyone warmly upon entering the room, especially Jenny. "Good afternoon, Jenny, how's my dear friend today."

Beaming from ear to ear and picking herself up in bed, Jenny replied, "Hi, Mother, thanks for coming again today. Dad,

Yo-Yo, Mother is the best card player ever, but she lets me win all the time." So, Mother and Jenny have met? More amazing was that Jenny called JR dad. That was especially heart-warming to hear. Mother glanced over to me with a slight grin to emphasize the little joke she played on me.

"No. No. Jenny is an awesome card player; I can't seem to beat her. She is always one step ahead of me."

Dad expressed his gratitude to Mother. "Thank you for all that you've done. Jenny glows after all your visits. We know you've spent a lot of time with her."

"Don't forget about me." Yo-Yo couldn't contain herself as she ran up and gave Mother one of her giant hugs, nearly knocking her over.

"Oh, what's this? How could I forget you? Never!" Mother's laughter was like a sweet melody that for a moment one could ignore where we were. "Now, I have to leave, but rest assured I'll be around. Michael, shall we leave to attend to other matters?"

"Yes, Mother, you have a busy schedule. I believe Yo-Yo's expression is *moustache*, isn't it?" Who knew the big fella had a sense of humor?

Once they gracefully exited the room, I turned to Jenny and

asked how she was feeling. The health of Jenny and my family was on mind. I needed closure that comes with the feeling of comfort that they would be safe and healthy going forward.

"I'm good. More importantly, how are you? I never adequately thanked you for saving me." Tears formed in her eyes as she tried to recount the pain and revelation of that night. "I felt lost for such a long time. It's like I was starring in one of those zombie movies, where I was wandering aimlessly along with my zombie friends through a desolate city. There was no hope for me, but you brought me back, even after all the bad things that happened to you and your family."

Dad was quick to correct her. "You mean our family because it includes you. It always will."

I was happy to hear Dad express his belief clearly and succinctly. Knowing that they would be forming their own trinity was immensely comforting to me. With Dad's fatherly attention and Yo-Yo's sisterly bond, Jenny would be in good hands, making my exit that much easier.

"Jenny, Dad is right. You have been through enough. Your glow is coming back and soon the whole world will see it. Happiness is an emotion that will never abandon you, because you have seen and lived the opposite way."

My dad then turned to me, wanting to talk further about

who or what I was now. "What do I call you now? Isaac? Jo-Jo? There's so much I want, we want, to say to you, or to ask you."

"Dad, you don't need to worry. Everything that I've been through has been worth it. I wandered through life, throwing my own pity party. All I needed to do was to focus on the beauty of life more and not the ugliness that often tries to capture our attention. My journey is just beginning. I hope I can make a difference for other people too."

We sat and reminisced for the rest of the afternoon, talking about comedic events in our lives. Dad reminded me of the Sundays working on the cars, often learning from mistakes, like the time we forgot to put motor oil in the GTO. That was an expensive lesson. Mom wasn't too happy with us that day. I reminded Yo-Yo of her war against the English language. Yo-Yo began to rub her temples and laugh as I recapped how some of her favorite words like Knight and night gave her a headache or words like presents and presence reduced her to comedic mental convulsions. "Remember, the time you stopped eating chicken because you heard it was fowl?"

"OK, rude." Yo-Yo couldn't stop laughing.

Jenny provided her own examples of happy times. Most involved sitting and gossiping with Yo-Yo. Other times involved me at school and how I tried to teach her science, with little success. The sparkle in her eyes and the glow in her face returned as we recounted the stories.

"Do you want to relive a moment again? I can take you there, all of us together." With some reluctance and a little prodding, they agreed. I asked them to join me close to Jenny's bed, with each taking a hand until we formed a circle. "Everyone, think of a special moment. Dad, you go first."

Dad's memory was of Mom, the day they first reclined together in that open pasture, staring up at the clouds. My mom's laughter and glow filled the memory for us all to see. Butterflies and birds flew against the backdrop of a radiantly blue sky, while the tall grass gently waved in a soft breeze, adding to the tapestry of the day. It was a memorable day.

Next was Yo-Yo, whose memory was her 10th birthday. It was a beautiful day. Our mom wasn't ill yet, but on that day, she had promised Yo-Yo a cake bigger than she ever had. We all spent the day helping Mom bake cakes that would become layered into our own version of the Leaning Tower of Pisa. Trying to eat it was funnier than the process to make it. We all laughed as it tumbled over after the first attempt was made to slice the cake. The table became our plate as we delighted in consuming this delicious dessert, each picking a part we liked. I preferred the vanilla piece of course, and Yo-Yo the chocolate cookie dough filling, while Mom and Dad fed each other the frosting. Finally, Mom would purposely smear the frosting on her beloved's face, to all our amusement. I had forgotten that day.

Jenny was last, but she resisted the offer, stating she didn't deserve a happy memory yet. Yo-Yo wouldn't take no for an answer. "C'mon, you know that's not true. Please do this for us."

Jenny then brought forward a memory that she had kept locked away. It was a day when she was very young, maybe five years old. It was a summer's day, one of the Saturday afternoon dates that Jenney shared with her father. Jenny always cherished those Saturdays with her dad, going to the movies and later devouring ice cream sundaes. She had just gone to a movie with her dad. They were talking about the silliness of the cartoon characters as they sat in a local ice cream parlor. Tried as she may, Jenny had some difficulty navigating the ice cream into her mouth. Mostly, it seemed to make a messy and sticky moustache and beard on her face. The vision of her dad, smiling at his baby and trying to clean her face, was the image of pure love that Jenny needed to see.

I wish the joy they felt that day could be bottled and shared with others, but there was one more vision I needed to show them before releasing them. It was the message that Mom gave me during the battle with Uncle Trick. Dad and Yo-Yo cried as they saw mom's message to them. I could have just told them what mom said. A visual, however, would remain with them forever. For my dad, I think seeing his beloved was the closure he needed.

For Yo-Yo, her tears of sadness alternated with tears of joy, as she knew that mom was with her still, even in death.

Released from their visions, they thanked me as they wiped tears from their eyes, with Yo-Yo crying to see mom one last time, while my dad held her tightly. It was now time to tell them that I was leaving and that my journey was larger than being home. The world was crying, yearning for help. If I could make a difference one person at a time, planting one small seed to flower and flourish, then perhaps that would be a good first step for charity and grace to grow exponentially.

My family wasn't thrilled to hear me talk about my pending departure, but they slowly accepted it. Yo-Yo was heartbroken at first. "You can't leave. What will we do without you?"

"Live! Live a long and happy life. The three of you are going to make an unbreakable team, together as one. Don't worry, I'll check in on you from time to time too."

After one last hug from them, I turned to leave. Dad followed me into the hallway. He wanted to tell me about Kat. He wasn't happy about her being the driving force in this tragic affair. He wasn't going to forgive her, but he wasn't going to let her affect the rest of his life. Kat, however, was getting her just punishment and perhaps someday she could have a semblance of a life, but not with them. Dad felt bonded to Jenny and wanted to keep her safe, like a father should. He just didn't feel the need to hate Kat, rather he pitied her. Mom was already dying when Kat hurried her demise along. Perhaps, she had unintentionally given my mother a quicker path to peace. Dad couldn't, however, forgive Kat for what she did to Jenny and me. A lack of forgiveness should not be compared to hate. While he could never forgive or condone her behavior, he accepted the truth and Kat's current punishment. Sometimes, that's the most we could expect. The way he saw it, acceptance allowed him to move forward with his life and to leave the past where it belongs, behind. Acceptance didn't mean approval.

Leaving the hospital, I reflected on what my father said. Separating the action from the person performing it is a difficult thing to do. The action occurred at a point in time, while the perpetrator was a constant reminder of the harm or injury inflicted on us. It is for our own benefit to separate the two, otherwise we would fall into a trap where hate and fear ruled. It has always been easier to remain victims of this trap, as it doesn't take a lot of effort to maintain a constant state of inertia. Standing while absorbing life's punches and rising back up after falling down have always been more difficult to do, but infinitely more rewarding.

If we don't try to extricate ourselves from the world's physical and spiritual traps, our essence is transformed. We are altered from a child-like state of looking at the world with innocent eyes to one that's jaundiced. Extricating ourselves from the trap gets more difficult as time passes, increasing its hold on us and our hold to past sins. The past becomes present and unchallenged.

Our continued growth was dependent on understanding and not hating history, our past, taking those lessons as specimens for study, nurturing the positives and acknowledging the negatives. A study of history offers a wonderful picture of people and life, with all the grandeur, successes, mistakes and frailties that are endemic to the human existence. Like my mom before me, I have come to embrace it.

CHAPTER 23

The next day, Captain and I arrived at the dock to sail off for our next adventure. I was still learning how we would know where to go and how the Fisherlady would get us there quickly. Normally, Captain would live on his boat. The house he kept locally was one of two he owned on land. He wouldn't tell me why, but he said he would always return to them. Evidently, the other was in Portugal. Perhaps, that's our next destination. He would only laugh when I asked him where we were going.

"Oh, Jo-Jo, you have only touched the surface of your power. On this voyage, I'll train you on your other abilities. Let's see how it goes."

As we were about to leave, Yo-Yo rushed down to the dock, wishing to say good-bye one more time. "Yo-Yo, what are you doing here?"

"I wanted to see you again and to hug Tres one more time."

Upon hearing her name and seeing Yo-Yo, Tres leaped from the boat and ran to her, laying kiss after kiss on my sister. It was a sight of pure joy that could never be forgotten.

The joy on both their faces convinced Captain that he needed to leave Tres with Yo-Yo. "Chiara, it seems you have won Tres' heart. Tres, do you agree?"

Tres response was clear; she barked and bounced happily from side to side. Yo-Yo gave her a big hug to show her how she felt about her.

With a smile on his face, Captain ordered Tres to stay with Yo-Yo. "Tres, you win girl. Now, you have to stay with Yo-Yo. Protect her and Jenny."

Tres barked her approval. After a hug from Yo-Yo to both Captain and me, we said our farewells. Thinking of his children as he gave my sister a gentle embrace, my new companion had a tear roll down his check. He patted me on the back and whispered fondly. "Tres is one lucky girl to have someone like Yo-Yo to love. I wish she could have met my children."

"Thanks for letting her stay. It means the world to me. At least, I know they'll be safe with Tres there."

Waving to my family from the boat, we pushed off to destinations unknown. "Moustache, Yo-Yo, moustache! I'll be back someday."

Turning my attention to Captain, I noticed he was holding something interesting. "Hey, what's that in your hand?"

"It's my rosary. I picked up a new pair. Mother did a number on me. This is part of my penance now. We all pick our way to show reverence to the Trinity. Mother holds it all together for me."

I shook my head and grinned at the revelation. "Captain, you'll never cease to amaze me. Never!"

Captain laughed uncontrollably as we exited the harbor. "Jo-Jo, prepare to be amazed a lot during our journey. Just wait until I tell you the story about the most powerful wraith. You are going to wet yourself when you hear who it is."

"Well, giddy-up."

Turning my attention to our lazy and inactive crew, who were standing a few feet away and staring at each other in confusion, I yelled, "Hey morons, the fish aren't going to catch themselves! Get the nets out!" By the way, Decker, Riley and T-Rex are now part of our crew. The Mannions have become Minions. We'll keep them around for a while.

The End......of the Beginning

PEACE AND LOVE TO ALL

Thanks for the visit.

Printed in Great Britain
by Amazon

26839212R00139